... University of
... her first novel, which won
...erty-Dunnan First Novel Prize.

Praise for *Lamb*

'Bonnie Nadzam manages to write gorgeous prose about people and skies and mountains while still creating tension and suspense on the level of a thriller, while also walking us into complex and delicate and unsettling moral territory with brilliant subtlety and insight. *Lamb* is a remarkable debut, by a writer to watch. I will be thinking about these characters for a long time.'

Aimee Bender, author of *The Particular Sadness of Lemon Cake*

'*Lamb* is one of the most powerful and original novels I have read in years. Beautiful, evocative, and brilliant.'

T.C. Boyle, author of *When the Killing's Done*

'[A] gripping psychological study ... This is a debut author who is definitely worth watching.'

The Herald

'This daring, disturbing first novel imagines the friendship of a child and an older man ... This debut novel ... flirts with the possibility that such relationships might not always have dire consequences ... This is a fiction of striking distinction.'

Independent

'This prize-winning and hugely impressive debut ... is a devastatingly convincing portrait of abuse, as the silver-tongued, self-pitying and sentimental Lamb remorselessly grooms the vulnerable child he has snatched from a Chicago street. It's stomach-twisting stuff, but when Lamb flees with Tommie in tow to the wide, wild prairies of the American West, the reader's dread is held in tension with scenic passages of lyrical beauty, to extraordinarily compelling effect. Add in pitch-perfect dialogue and this utterly assured, high-stakes, high-wire act of a novel is proof that Nadzam is a very special talent indeed.'

Daily Mail

'I barely took a breath as I raced through this taut, compulsively readable book ... *Lamb* won prizes when it was published in America last year and it's easy to see why. It's a bold book ... gradually, with the page-turning suspense of a thriller Nadzam reveals Lamb: a damaged, destructive man anaesthetising himself against a tragic childhood, failed marriage and imploding career ... He is a haunting creation, to be both pitied and despised. This daring book will stay with you for days.'

Sunday Telegraph

'A disturbing tale of manipulation and self-delusion as an older man forges a relationship with a young girl ... This is a brilliantly unsettling read that casts a dark, manipulative spell – particularly against the gorgeously described backdrop of the American West.'

Marie Claire

'Unsettling, suspenseful ... A morbidly fascinating debut; Nadzam's beautiful prose makes the flesh creep.'

Financial Times

'This tale should be one that makes the reader feel nothing but repulsion; that it doesn't is the beauty of this debut novel ... As their friendship develops, it becomes increasingly difficult to see their situation in black and white, making for an unsettling and challenging read.'

Psychologies

'Only an immensely promising young writer could bestow such grace on such troubled characters.'

Boston Globe

'Surprisingly tender, highly inappropriate ... Nadzam deserves credit for her convincing portrait of a middle-aged male burnout ... [Lamb] is difficult and beautiful, and though it may not be normal, it feels very real.'

Time Out New York

'Lolita gets a 21st-century spin in this gripping debut ... Nadzam has a crisp, fluid writing style, and her dialogue is reminiscent of Sam Shepard's ... it's a fine first effort: storytelling as accomplished as it is unsettling.'

Publishers Weekly

Lamb

Bonnie Nadzam

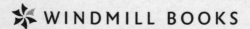
WINDMILL BOOKS

Published by Windmill Books 2013

2 4 6 8 10 9 7 5 3 1

Copyright © Bonnie Nadzam 2011

Published by arrangement with Other Press, New York

First published in Great Britain in 2012 by Hutchinson

Windmill Books
The Random House Group Limited
20 Vauxhall Bridge Road, London SW1V 2SA

Addresses for companies within The Random House Group Limited can be found at:
www.randomhouse.co.uk/offices.htm

The Random House Group Limited Reg. No. 954009

www.randomhouse.co.uk

A CIP catalogue record for this book
is available from the British Library

ISBN 9780099558927

The Random House Group Limited supports the Forest Stewardship
Council® (FSC®), the leading international forest-certification organisation.
Our books carrying the FSC label are printed on FSC®-certified paper. FSC is
the only forest-certification scheme supported by the leading environmental
organisations, including Greenpeace. Our paper procurement policy
can be found at: www.randomhouse.co.uk/environment

Printed and bound by CPI Group (UK) Ltd, Croydon, CR0 4YY

For Carrie, Chrissie, Mom, and Dad

Darkness is light; do not see it as light.

LAMB

We'll say this all began just outside of Chicago, in late summer on a residential street dead-ending in a wall. It was the kind of wall meant to hide freeways from view, and for miles in each direction parallel streets ended at the same concrete meridian. No trees on the lawn, no birds on wires. Northern shrikes gone, little gray-bellied wrens gone. Evening grosbeaks and elm trees and most of the oaks and all the silver brooms of tall grass and bunch flowers and sweetfern and phlox gone. Heartsease gone. About the tops of upturned trash bins, black flies scripted the air.

Imagine the corner house made of white brick and aluminum siding the color of yellow mud. Inside an old man sat in a dim-lit television room, tipped back in his La-Z-Boy, a box of microwaved chicken balanced on his sunken chest. He had shuffled into the yellow kitchen and taken a vacuum-packed meal from the freezer out of habit, microwaved and carried it with a sour dishrag into the TV room out of habit. It wasn't until he sat down and smelled it that he remembered he'd intended not to eat. He let it cool and he picked at it with his fingers. Tried not to breathe. Again and again he held his breath until some will that was not his own reclaimed it.

The front door opened and the old man started. A thin spot of saliva glistened at the corner of his mouth.

"Dad." The door shut and David Lamb walked into the kitchen and set his keys on the table. "Christ, Dad. It stinks in here." He paused for a moment in the kitchen doorway. A trail of ants ran beneath his shoe like a liquid crack in the filthy linoleum.

The old man looked down at his cold, rubbery lunch in its cardboard dish. David Lamb opened the collar of his fine baby blue shirt and stepped into the TV room. He picked up the box off the old man's chest and set it down on the table. "Didn't I call to have someone clean this place up last week? Didn't she come?"

The old man reached for the remote and squinted across the room at the television screen.

"You sleeping down here, Dad?"

"Stairs are giving me a pain in the ass."

"You should have called me. We could move a bed downstairs."

"I don't want any goddamned bed in here."

"What about that twin bed?"

The old man straightened and raised his voice, ropy with mucus. "Where's Cathy? She gone? Did you get fired?"

"No, I didn't get fired."

"She dead?"

"No, Cathy isn't dead."

The old man held himself erect, then sank back in his chair and waved a ragged hand in Lamb's direction. "I'm going to die watching TV."

"Let's go see a movie. Or get some burgers at Cy's. You want to?"

"Leave me alone. You don't want to take me out. I can tell."

"Don't you want something decent to eat, Dad? You have something in the freezer?"

"What are you doing here? You get fired?"

"No, Dad."

"Your wife die too? What was she, drunk driving?"

"Cathy is fine. Let's eat something."

"You never wanted to make me dinner. I could tell."

"Always made you dinner, Dad."

"Thirty-five years ago last week she died. You didn't even notice the day."

"Sure I did."

"September third."

"I know it, Dad."

"Thirty-five."

"I know."

"Like hell you do."

David turned away. Out the window the last of the grimy daylight glanced off passing cars in the street. "Back of her white blouse as she steps down the front stairs and out to her car. One little suitcase in her hand."

"Ana didn't bring any goddamned suitcase with her. What. Like she knew what was going to happen? Her grocery bag. Maybe she had her grocery bag but she sure as hell didn't have any suitcase."

"In her blue jeans. Black hair shining down her back. Drives off in the car I bought her. Leaves the bracelet I bought her in London."

"London? London? Let me tell you about getting old. I'll tell you about getting old."

"There she goes, chin up. Off to find some other, decent man."

"She was an angel, David. She was an angel."

"Dad."

"Oh, for Christ's sake, would you leave me alone."

"I need to ask you something."

"Bullshit you do."

"Father to son."

"Leave me alone. I got no answers."

"Okay. Okay." Lamb stood. "Let me make you some dinner. You have anything decent around here?" He went back to the kitchen, opened the freezer.

"I don't want anything decent. If I wanted anything decent I'd want meat loaf. And I don't have any ground meat in there."

"Sure you do, Dad."

"All I want is a little meat loaf. And a little gin. Is that too much to ask? For a miserable man who's dying all alone?"

"Have anything green? Green peas? How's that?"

"Leave me alone. Can't you see I'm dying?"

"Peas it is."

"Get the hell out of my house."

David Lamb shut the freezer, picked up a gold can of beer from a half-empty box on the counter, and sat at the kitchen table.

"Peas," his father said. "Who eats peas."

"I guess we never did." He opened the beer.

"Nobody to buy us fucking peas."

David stared out the dirty glass window. "No," he said, "there sure wasn't."

And we'll say it was that same early evening and fifteen miles away in one dingy bedroom of a concrete apartment building by the freeway where the girl cut the neck, shoulders, and sleeves off a ratty purple shirt, held it up to her chest to assess herself in the mirror leaning against the wall, and cut five inches from the bottom. She was turning side to side in faded floral underwear and the wrecked T-shirt when the door opened. She snatched at her jeans on the floor and held them up to cover herself. The man stood in the entryway and looked at her and snorted. "What's that supposed to be?"

The girl was silent.

"When I was a kid, an adult asked me a question, I answered."

"A shirt." Her voice was grainy and low.

"A shirt." The man nodded. "It doesn't look like much of a shirt."

"I'm getting dressed."

He stepped back into the hall and pulled the door with him. "That's not going to stay up on you." He talked through the flimsy wooden divide.

"I know that." She held her pants over her underwear and bare legs and the remnant of purple shirt slipped down her narrow freckled body. Her limbs were pale and wiry, and she had a little belly on her, and no waist, cage of her ribs jammed close to her hips. Pointy elbows, pointy knees. "Where's my mom?"

"Late."

"What's for dinner?"

"Cap'n Crunch."

"I don't want cereal for dinner."

"Yeah, well, neither do I."

The girl looked at her desk, her orange backpack. "I have homework."

"Bullshit you're doing homework. Put on a real shirt and come out here."

"When is she coming home?"

"Later."

"Oh."

"Come on. You gotta eat." She could hear his heavy footfalls on the mashed, gravy-colored carpet as he went back toward the kitchen. Her back to the door, she stepped out of the shirt, retrieved a pink stapler from her desk drawer, and stapled the inside seams and uneven hems.

· · · · ·

At the funeral, Lamb watched alone as they lowered a sealed casket into a deep, empty rectangle framed by artificial turf. It seemed to him there was neither father nor burial involved. Afterward he parked his truck in the lot between a liquor barn and a dollar store and stood by the bus-stop bench in his black suit and dead father's Cubs hat, an unlit cigarette between his lips. He scanned the horizon and the ground for something green, for a place where he could press his cheek against warm grass or dirt, for anything like a loophole, a chink, a way out. Nothing before him but the filthy street and bright signs announcing the limits of his world: Transmission Masters and Drive Time Financing and Drive-Thru Liquors and Courtesy Loans and Office Depot and a Freeway Inn and a Luxury Inn and a Holiday Inn. If there was something beneath, something behind, it was hidden from him. Even his father had been hemmed in, jarred off, sewn up. They'd sewn his lips together.

In the story that was his life even just a summer ago—God—a thing can get only so big before it dismantles itself, as if in accord with some inarticulable law of the universe everyone knows but unwittingly forgets. Even in places as small and clean as a newly remodeled kitchen in eggshell white and stainless steel, it was true. Granite countertops, beveled glass gilded from the outside by light at the end of day; two fingers of gin in a tumbler; newspapers and mail piling up on the island in the kitchen; Cathy in gold eyeglasses trimming the tapered ends of French green beans; Elizabeth Draper's blue necklace of tiny glass beads in his silk-lined pants pocket; Linnie ringing his cell phone; his cuff links flashing every time he lifts his glass; a fax coming in from Wilson; nightly news from the flat-screen in the sunken living room; John Draper grinning sheepishly at the door wanting him out on the driveway or in the garage for a beer; Cathy's sister bleary-eyed and wrinkled pulling up in her Volvo: hi, David. All of that, and what was there now to hold him up?

Lamb rubbed his temple and thought he might sit down right there in the parking lot, wait to see who'd come for him or who would ask him to move, but when he turned away from the wake of traffic to light the cigarette, he saw the girl.

She was coming toward him in a lopsided purple tube top and baggy shorts and brass-colored sandals studded with rhinestones. She carried a huge pink patent-leather purse and was possibly the worst thing he'd seen all day. Scrawny white arms and legs stuck out of her clothes. The shorts hung around her pelvic bones and her stomach stuck out like a dirty spotted white sheet. It was grotesque. It was lovely. Freckles concentrated in bars across her cheekbones and down the tiny ridge of her nose and the slightest protruding curve of her forehead just above her eyebrows. There were huge freckles, pea sized, and smaller ones. Some faint, others dark, overlapping like burnt confetti on her bare shoulders and nose and cheeks. He stared at her. He had never seen anything like it.

"Hi." She had a little gap between her front teeth, and her eyes were wide set, and she had one of those noses with perfectly round nostrils. She was a pale little freckled pig with eyelashes. "I'm supposed to ask you for a cigarette."

Behind her, huddled near the trash can up against the brick wall of the CVS, two girls were watching in a bright little knot of bangles and short shorts and ponytails. He looked at the girl. Her chewed and ratty fingernails. Her small feet in shoes two or three sizes too big for her. Her mother's shoes, he supposed. He felt a little sick.

"What is this?" he said. "Some kind of dare?"

The girl tipped her head, put her hand up to her eyes to shield the sun.

"What grade are you in?"

"Seventh."

"Don't they teach you anything?"

She shrugged. Behind her the girls were laughing.

"Was this your idea?"

Shrug.

"Whose was it?"

"Sid's."

"Which one is she?"

The girl turned around and her friends became suddenly still. "The one on the right," she said.

"The blonde."

"Yeah."

"Sid like Sidney."

"Yeah."

Sid knew she was being studied. She pushed back her hair and stuck out her hip.

"She in seventh grade too?"

"We all are."

"She looks older."

"I know."

David Lamb reached into his pocket for the cigarettes. He looked up at the cameras above the CVS, cameras that were pointed at the doors and at the parking lot. He shook one out and gave it to her. She turned back toward her friends with the cigarette in her hand and giggled.

"Well, go on," he said. "Put it in your mouth and I'll light it. A lady doesn't light her own cigarette." She put it between her lips and raised her eyebrows. "That's it. Now steady. Don't look at the cigarette, look at me," he said, touching the lit end of his own cigarette to hers. "Inhale. Go on. Draw it in." He straightened and she puffed.

"Now," he said, "what do I get in exchange?"

She held the half-lit cigarette between two fingers and wrinkled her forehead. "I don't have anything."

The girl looked uneasy. She lifted her hand, as if to offer back the cigarette.

"No money?"

She shook her head.

"What's in that purse?"

She lifted it a little, remembering it. "Makeup," she said. "Nothing." Her eyes darted sideways, as if she knew she was in a place she shouldn't be. Behind her the blond girl said something to the other, and they laughed. This ugly kid before Lamb obviously the brunt of their joke. Stupid. And reckless. Had they any idea who he was? Why he was standing there alone in a black suit? What kind of heart, if any, hung inside him? And how was this not a joke on him? He took a long pull on his own cigarette and put it out on the bottom of his beautiful polished shoe. The girl watched him flick out the last shreds of tobacco and put the soiled filter in his pants pocket. There was no wind, no birds, no one calling. The sky hung low and white and warm like the ghost of something.

"Don't you wish you'd been born sooner?" he said, looking over her head at the grease-stained asphalt. The freckled girl watched him take the cigarette from her hand, ash it, and return it to her fingers. She meant to go back now—but she leaned back a little on her heels, staring up at him.

"Tell me something. Do your friends frequently put you up to things like this?"

"I guess."

He nodded down at his suit. "I just buried my father."

"Oh."

"Ever been to a wake?"

She scrunched up her nose at him.

"It's like a funeral."

She shook her head. He studied the part in her hair. Pink stripe of skin through hair so pale it was almost white. "Listen," he told the girl, "your friends are laughing at you. You know that, don't you?"

She pulled up the sides of her purple top, one side at a time. It slipped down.

"I'm going to give you a tip, okay? A favor."

She shrugged and lifted her fingers as if to say: but you already gave me the cigarette.

"No," he said, "this is something you're not going to forget. I'll give you this whole pack of cigarettes, okay?" He took them out of his pocket and made a big show of dropping them into her purse. Her friends were watching now. He had their attention. "In exchange, you let me play a trick on your friends. On Sid. Teach her a lesson."

"I don't know." She squinted her eyes. "What kind of trick?"

"Let's scare them."

"How?"

He took the girl's bare arm just above the elbow and she jerked back, as if suddenly awake. Everything quickened. The sky seemed brighter, traffic faster. "Let's pretend," he said low, talking fast, already pulling her toward his Ford, "that I'm kidnapping you. I'm going to pull you, just like this—" She dropped the cigarette and tripped over the long ends of the sandals. "And I'm going to walk you to my car," he said, pulling her along. "You're not going to scream, but you're going to look back at them. Okay? So they know you're afraid." Inadvertently the girl did exactly as he said. "Now don't freak out," he said. "We're just scaring your friends. They deserve it, right? I'm not going to hurt you."

"No," she started. "Wait." He opened the driver's side of the navy blue Explorer and lifted and sort of pushed her over into the passenger seat. It was all done in less than ten seconds. She smacked her head against the window and cried out.

"I'm teaching you a lesson, right?"

She put her hands against the inside of the window and looked at her friends, who stood frozen, the ends of their ponytails hung limp in the thin air.

Lamb pulled the door shut and locked it and started the engine. "You're not hurt, are you?" She shrank against the door, holding her head. "I'm taking you home," he said. "I'm just taking you home. What's your address?" She faced the window and pulled on the door handle again and again and again, knocked and knocked, and she looked back at him over her shoulders. Her eyes were huge. Then they were free and clear, out of the parking lot and onto the four-lane.

"Where do you live?" he raised his voice, gained speed. "Tell me which way." They passed a KFC, a BP. She told him in a trembling voice and he repeated it, pointing over the tops of the stores to three apartment buildings. The girl nodded. He scolded her the whole way, playing it angry. His hands were shaking on the wheel. The backs of his thighs wet. He yelled at her like he thought a father would have done.

"I could be taking you somewhere to kill you. You know that?"

She clung to the door on her side.

"It was a dumb thing to do, coming up to me like that. Wasn't it?"

She pulled at the handle again and again.

"Say something."

"I'm sorry," the girl whispered. "Please." She was terrified. Well, good. It was true, what he'd said. He could be taking her off to kill her. He could do anything he wanted. Her lips drew in toward her gapped teeth. "Now just stop it," he said. "Just stop it." And when he saw where she lived, near the freeway behind a gas station off six lanes of traffic—and for the second time in the minutes since she'd first approached him—a feeling of pity for her was eclipsed by the shock of knowing he, too, was on the losing end of all this. After all, here he was. It was a moment they were trapped in together.

"Don't let your friends push you around like that," he said. She stared at him and tugged on the door handle. "And put some clothes on." He looked her up and down. "I mean, what are you supposed to be? Who decided you were going to be this way—all stupid and . . . dressed like that?"

"Please," she whispered. She was white.

"Now wait," he said and pulled into the square lot before the entrance of her building. He unlocked the doors and she fell out. "Wait a minute," he said. He had her purse and waved it. "Keys?"

She crawled up onto her feet and stepped away from the car, a body's length away, and looked at the purse.

"Give it to me!"

"Now wait a minute."

"Calling the police!" Her voice was shrill. Lamb glanced around. It was an accusation. A warning. But only because she was humilated. Lamb saw her taking it all in: his expensive suit, the Ford Explorer, the leather seats, his clean haircut, his smooth face, everything clean, everything expensive, everything easy. He handed her the purse and she took out the cigarettes and threw them at him.

"I'm not a bad guy," he said. "But I could have been."

Her eyes were lit up with hate.

"Good," Lamb said. "That's good." There was some little filament of heat in this girl that he had not expected, and he was relieved to see it, relieved to be surprised by something. By anything. Across from the apartment building a traffic light turned green and a car honked and the traffic moved again. A middle-aged man with a huge gut and a brown mustache stood at the glass doors watching them.

"Maybe I should come in and tell your folks what happened," he said.

"Nobody's home." Of course they weren't.

"You have sisters? Brothers?"

"I have friends." She flung her words like stones.

"That's right," Lamb said, nodding. "You think they went in that drugstore to tell someone what happened?"

She looked at him, her eyes reducing back to their stupid blue. "No."

"Me eithcr."

He watched her face fall. He knew what that was. He knew about the room she was shrinking into. "I could make up any old story to tell them," she said.

He thought about it. Imagined what the stories could be. He looked at her bare arms and legs, her stapled, makeshift tube top slipping down her narrow chest. "Tell them I took you shopping."

"Oh, that's good."

"Okay, then."

"Okay. Bye."

They looked at each other a second, two, and she stepped away, slammed the door shut. She turned and walked up to the building. A latchkey kid. The sort who got C's in school. Not a pretty kid, not an athletic kid, not a smart kid. Just a skinny, slow-blooming kid desperate to keep up with her friends. Quick to make new ones. Stupid. Maybe she'd learned something today. Maybe he'd done her a favor. What'd it matter? Girl like her.

$$\cdot\ \cdot\ \cdot\ \cdot\ \cdot$$

That wasn't kidnapping. It had been a favor, right? A lesson. He hadn't kidnapped anyone. She was back in her apartment, having dinner with her parents, her girlfriends perhaps chastened of whoring each other out for laughs in parking lots. It wasn't kidnapping when the kid ended up safely delivered home in better shape than she left in the morning. It was like he found a loose bolt out there in the world and had carefully turned it back into place. It was fine.

It was six. He was back in the Residence Inn. Across the hall was another man, just like him. Both their beautiful houses for sale. Both their aging wives back on the market. He and this other guy—they even had the same haircut, the same belly just beginning to roll over the same beautiful leather belt. Why was it everywhere he looked he saw an incomplete version of himself? What was he supposed to do? Complete this stranger across the hall? Why was everything such a riddle?

He was supposed to call Linnie, drive her north along the lake. Spaghetti. Ribs. And walk until they felt the bite of October coming over the water, her eyes an unreal green in the dark. An expensive and well-educated system of reactions and responses, and he knew them all. Had known them, frankly, since years before she was born.

Damp from the shower, he sat on the edge of the hotel bed in his towel, traffic shushing and the light failing. There was room service: the Caesar, the salmon, the spinach omelet; the steakhouse nearby that would deliver; the sort of French café down the street that'd be empty—he could have a table alone and not be bothered. Or he could find someone to bother him. He took shallow breaths, his thoughts quick images of prepared food, of his father's translucent hand, himself as he'd looked at nineteen, all his hair dark, Linnie's young naked body from the front, the back, another plate of food with french fries on it, one image superimposed upon another until suddenly he felt the phone in his hand.

He called Cathy. He didn't expect an answer, but he'd hear at least her recorded voice. He wanted to hear that. But on the telephone was no recorded voice, no cheerful greeting—only the broken succession of minor notes signaling that he'd dialed the wrong number, that the number had been disconnected or changed. He paused, closed the phone, and lay back, setting it on his bare chest. His face heated and reddened and he lay still, absorbing the shock of it. This was September. This was going to be their second courting period. He was going to win her back. Linnie would be off with some other slick young guy. Everything would be all knit up by Thanksgiving. The house would fail to sell, and everything back the way it was before. She would forgive him. She always did. They'd build a fire and wear long pajamas and drink tea and she would touch the sides of his face and he would be sorry. And she would forgive him.

He sat up, opened the phone, and dialed the girl. "Linnie. It's me. Yeah yeah, I know. I know." He was whispering. "I'm sorry, baby. What? Listen. I can't talk long. Cathy's downstairs." His eyes watered and the darkening hotel room smeared. "Oh, stop it. That's not true. Linnie. I swear, okay? God's honest truth." He spoke very quietly. A man and woman passed outside his hotel room door. "Listen," he said, "I'm lying here naked on the bed." He gathered himself in his hand and asked her if she'd talk to him. Five or six minutes. And he promised her they'd have another weekend soon. Yes, Cathy would be going out of town, he'd get them a room somewhere, and he turned his head sideways to rest the phone against his shoulder and he took himself in both hands.

After he hung up he turned on the TV, then off, and sat up with his towel in his lap. It was dark outside the windows now and he watched his naked reflection in the glass as he dressed. He went alone into the mauve and beige bar downstairs, for a drink. He had three. He couldn't get the kid out of his head. He hoped he hadn't hurt her. He hadn't exactly been thinking clearly. But he hadn't meant to hurt her. He was not that kind of man.

. . . . .

In the middle of the workday at the small firm where he'd worked with Wilson for the last nineteen years, Lamb took his father's ball cap from the empty chair by his office door and left. He drove through the city, through the warm and thickening haze, returning to the same dim parking lot where he had seen the girl twenty-four hours before. He set himself at the bus stop and was not surprised when he saw her coming down the gummy sidewalk minutes later, in long sleeves and pants despite the heat. Somehow—how?—he'd known she would come. He always knew everything. Nothing in the world ever surprised him anymore, ever. Imagine that. Feeling that.

"Did you come back for cigarettes?" he asked. "Because I've quit since yesterday. I'm on a new plan."

No response. Arms crossed, mouth a thin puckered line.

"Shouldn't you be in school?"

"I left."

"Was that a good idea?"

"None of them even called me," she said. "To see if you'd killed me or what." Her words made the air tight around them.

Lamb frowned. "I'm sorry," he said. "I really am."

She sat down on the bench, half an arm's length away from him. "And after first period? Sid said hey, I heard about what you did with that guy yesterday. She said everybody was talking about it." The girl looked over at him. "She meant you."

"How do you know she meant me? Did she describe me?"

The girl rolled her eyes.

"No," he said. "I mean it. Did she get a really good look at me? Because in case you didn't notice"—he turned his head this way, then that, so the girl could see his profile on each side—"I'm really old."

She almost smiled.

"Listen," he said. He scanned her up and down. "I'm glad to see you've covered yourself up."

She stared at him.

"What's your name?"

"Tommie."

"Tommie?"

"You want to make fun of my name too?"

"It's a beautiful name."

"No it isn't."

"Sure it is."

She shrugged and hugged herself.

"Listen, Tommie. I'm sorry if your friends are being nasty. It feels like I'm to blame, doesn't it?"

Nothing.

"But look. Here we both are, right?"

Nod.

"Why did you come back here?"

"I don't know."

"I thought about you yesterday," he said. "I was worried I'd hurt you."

She stared at the curb.

"Can I tell you something?"

"What."

"I've never seen freckles like yours before. I apologize for staring."

"They're fugly." She glanced up at him.

"Well. I don't know what that means but I don't like the sound of it. And I myself happen to think they're striking. Stunning. And you know what else?"

"What."

"I'm an expert on freckles."

She smiled. "Sounds like the kind of dumb thing my mom would say."

"Look at me. I might be a lot of things, but I'm not a liar, okay?"

"Okay."

"There's precious little truth in this world, and I am one of its most enthusiastic spokespeople. Okay?"

"Okay."

He closed his eyes and tipped back his head. "I think," he said, "there's still some life running beneath these streets." The girl said nothing. He looked at her. "Your friends are just scared, you know. Scared and stupid."

She shrugged. "Not really my friends anymore."

"Were they good friends?"

"I guess."

"You've known them since you were kids? Little kids? You've lived here your whole life in this neighborhood?"

The girl nodded.

"I'm sorry to hear that." He turned to her. "Look at that face," he said. "Your face needs a line of broken-toothed mountains behind it. A girl like you needs a swimming hole. A river. Trees and clear skies. Ever go fishing? Or camping or hunting?"

"With who?"

"With anybody."

"No."

"Your mom buys you meat from the grocery store?"

"Yeah."

"On little white Styrofoam trays?"

"Yeah."

"Don't say yeah, say yes."

"Yes."

"You've never wrestled an animal to the ground and cut out his heart and eaten him in the dark, by a fire?"

The girl half smiled.

"Did you ever go camping?"

"Like sleeping outside?"

"Like sleeping outside."

"No."

"What about Dad?"

"Good question."

"Uncles?"

"Nope."

"I'm thinking of taking a sort of camping trip."

"Oh."

"Did you tell your mother about yesterday?"

"No way."

"You think she'd freak out."

"I don't know what she'd do."

"You didn't say anything because you were embarrassed. Is that it?"

The girl shrugged. A bus sped up to the curb, brakes hissing and screeching. She leaned back from it. The tall paneled doors folded open. No one stepped on or off. The doors shut and the bus drove away. "What's your name anyway?"

He looked at her. "Gary."

"I'm glad it's not Tom."

"That would be too weird."

"We couldn't be friends."

He checked his watch. "Listen. I need to make an appearance at work again. You want some lunch and I'll take you home?"

"Yesterday you said I shouldn't go up to strangers."

"But you just did."

"Oh."

"You're a little stubborn, aren't you?"

"Yeah," she said. "Yes."

"You know something, you're practically the only living person I know."

She scrunched up her nose. "What are you talking about?"

"Come on," he said "I won't drag you this time. Your own free will. Let me get you lunch. It's my way of apologizing if I scared you."

"You didn't scare me."

"Yes I did."

"It was pretty stupid."

"You or me?"

"Both."

"Smart girl."

"You're not going to take me back to school?"

"Not if you don't want to go."

"Just lunch and home?"

"Lunch and home. We'll do a drive-through. Your choice."

"Really?"

"Come on." The girl stood. "We're sort of getting to know each other, aren't we?"

At the drive-through he felt worse. It was the cheapness of the food, the unwholesomeness of it. He wondered how long the meat in her sandwich had been dead, or if someone behind the counter had spit in it, or not washed their hands before assembling it, and where the chicken had been raised and killed and by whom and for what recompense. The kid couldn't know what she was missing, the depths to which she was being duped by a world she had no hand in making. She needed something else to steer by. Something other than this. A person who—as it turned out—had both the inclination and resources to do so. It wasn't anything noble, or grand. He just wanted to do the little things for her, promise her a decent a meal someday soon. "With a glass of milk," he said. "And grilled cheese and a fresh sliced pear," he said. "How about that?"

"My grandma used to make those. She called it toasted cheese. Cut them in triangles."

"Oh, that's good. And did she ever grill it for you outside? Like on a little camping stove by a river?"

"My grandma? Who never even wore pants?"

"Someday we'll do that. You and me."

"Good luck finding a river."

"I know some rivers."

He brought her back to the apartment building, pulled into the lot, and took his sandwich and carton of fries out of the paper sack. "Here," he said. "You take the bag." He nodded at the security guard through the windshield, a dumpy-looking kid with a smear of facial hair beneath his nose.

"If you want," Tommie said, "I could give you my e-mail or something."

"Why? Are we meeting again?"

Her face went blank. She had the most vacant, stupid expression when she wasn't angry. Extraordinary skin, speckled little piglet skin, but no lights on behind it. He had a sudden impulse to strike her, print her with a bruise in the shape of his hand. Put something behind her face. Make her shriek. Hear something wild and untempered come out of her. Hadn't there been some little rage in her an hour ago? And was there no way to rouse it again?

"Want to know something?" He looked at her dim eyes. "I don't exactly have any friends in this town."

"That makes two of us."

• • • • •

They met ten times in the next week, before school and after. He fed her a little something every time: sliced her an apple with his pocketknife, drove her all the way into the city for a street dog and a pretzel. He brought her little things from the boxes of precious junk from his father's house: a silver can opener for soda bottles, a little book of hand-drawn North American birds. He brought her a white paper bag of cut licorice to put under her pillow to sneak after midnight and a heavy pocket-sized pencil sharpener made of solid silver—something she could reach into her pocket and hold on to when Sid or Jenny or anyone else was nearby or whispering across the room. She made it early to the bus stop every morning and he picked her up and brought her to a pancake house and still delivered her on time to first period, her belly full of blueberries and sausage.

Eventually, when it seemed time, he took her for a whole day. "We don't want any trouble, we don't want any worry. So we have to plan carefully," he'd said. "Right?"

And so they had. He drove her in his Ford past the Fox River and into the prairie reserves and green and muddy ponds beyond. It was a day suddenly hot and clear. The weather like summer again—a lie of lies when the first of autumn's cool rainy mornings had already begun. The day itself drowsy in the honeyed light, as if space itself were drained of the energy it took to sustain such falsehood.

"Do you want me to tell you about it? How it will be on the other side of Nebraska?" He handed her a cold orange-and-silver can of soda and she leaned her head against the inside of the rear window frame, skinny bare legs stretched out along the tailgate behind him. His blue shirtsleeves were rolled to the elbows and he stood leaning against the truck, his new boots crossed in the dirt. It was hot. Nothing moved. Where he'd parked, the narrow road was split with a high stripe of needlegrass and thistles. I-80 hummed behind them. He took off his father's baseball cap and wiped his forehead on his forearm.

The girl snorted and opened her soda, a fine spray of mist.

"I can take you home if you're just going to snort at me, miss piggy."

"No no. I'm listening."

"Are you going to interrupt?"

"No."

He reached over and, without touching her, ran his palm close before her face. "You have to close your eyes. Are you ready?"

"Ready."

"Keep your eyes closed."

"I am."

He sat opposite her on the tailgate, his legs stretched out alongside hers, his boots at her hip. He cracked open his own soda; it hissed. "This is out in a high, wide valley," he said. "Okay? Really high. Thousands of feet."

"Okay."

"Can you see it?" He paused, drinking. "Acres of pale grass. Almost gray. Big knots of silver brush. We call that sage."

"I know that."

"Good. Picture that. And one house. A little one, whitewashed. A slash of dark green half a mile off where the cottonwoods and tamarack grow by the river. Can you see all of that?"

"Yes."

"Do you know why it's half a mile off?"

"Why?"

"In case it floods."

"Oh."

"There's only this one road, the Old El Rancho Road, and it's still unpaved. It's locked behind a cattle gate you have to open with a little black key."

"I like that."

"I know you do. Beside the little triangle house there's a shop, with a woodstove, and an old AM radio, and all my father's old tools, and his old arc welder, and the table saw. A freezer full of hot dogs and a cooler full of Mexican beer. On the workbench is a giant glass pickle jar filled with old nails. Beside that, a little tin box where I'll keep half a pack of cigarettes. But you're not allowed to have any."

The girl smiled, eyes closed, the cold can sweating between her bare thighs. He looked at her short blue cotton shorts. Doll clothes. He measured her up with his eyes as he talked, her arms and shoulders and wrist bones. God, she was small.

"Just off the back of the shop, there'll be a smaller room, with a bright rug of braided rags on the concrete floor. You know the kind? Kind of a country rug, right?"

"Yes."

"This room stays real cool in the summertime. Inside there's a set of bunk beds. Soft old sleeping bags open on them. A metal nightstand beside the lower bunk with a couple of books on it, right? Your bird book. And a water glass. In the spring, when it's warm enough, we'll move out to this little room. And I'll sleep on the bottom bunk, and you'll sleep on the top, next to the small sliding window that looks out over the water tank for the old ragged brown horse we keep. And Tommie, let me tell you something: this is a horse you really love. Beyond that, just road and high grass and more high grass, and shadows of low clouds racing over the ground, and far out there will be the range, purple and blue, a long jagged bruise across the palest stripe of sky. And sometimes, if from the bottom bunk I call up to you, will you lean over the edge of the bed with your round shoulders, and let your hair hang down, and say oh hello, you."

"Sure."

"I know you will. You'll be so good to me. I'll be all old and gray and all the sturdy young men on the plain will be in love with you. They'll come by on their motorcycles or in their fast cars and they'll have dark shining hair and straight white teeth and they'll be tall and beautiful. You have to promise me you'll go with them."

The girl snorted.

"And I'll fry you eggs early in the morning, and butter you a thick piece of cold bread, and I'll slice the bacon myself, and bring you hot chocolate, and you'll sit on the wood rail fence in your nightgown, and I'll put my jacket over your shoulders, and we'll balance our plates on our knees and watch the sun come up while we eat. And when I have to leave the house to go to work you'll wait for me, won't you? You'll sit on the fence and watch the dirt road till you see me coming back home to you."

"Will you be on the old horse?"

"Oh, you sweet girl. I'll *be* that horse. Look at me. I am that sad old horse. I'll come stumbling up the edge of the road. So tired. But if you put your face very close, here, to my breath—here, closer, like that—and if you listen carefully, you'll hear me whisper. Come up. Let's go get the world while there's still some of it worth getting."

They sat very still.

"You want to?"

She opened her eyes. "Yes."

"Okay?"

"You mean really?"

"I mean really. Ready or not. How long do you need to pack?"

She grinned. "Oh please," she said. "About one minute."

He tipped back his soda and went aaaaahhhhh and grinned at her. "Wouldn't it be fun if we could?"

"Can't we?"

"Of course not, stupid."

• • • • •

The dear girl. How could she not carry Lamb with her, all the grassy fields he painted hanging between her little face and the world, bright screens printed with the images he made for her: flashes of green and silver; huge birds circling in the wind; the wet brown eye of a horse; yellow eggs on a breakfast dish; the curve of their backs atop a weathered rail fence on a cool blue morning.

When she returned home the night after their tailgate picnic, it was almost dark. Lamb watched her go in and wait in the dirty yellow light for the steel elevator doors to open. She'd travel up the nine floors with a skinny boy whose face was lumpy and red with acne. He lived on fourteen. He wore skinny black jeans and a silver chain from his front pocket to the back. He might smirk and point his eyes at Tommie like he was hungry, and didn't she know what for?

"What happened to your face?" he would ask her. "Did someone put a colander over your head and spray diarrhea on you?" He crossed his hands behind his head and leaned back against the metal wall. "I have a special lotion that'll take them off. If you want me to spread some of it on you."

Tommie would stare ahead until the boy spat across the car to the dented steel wall upon which she'd fixed her gaze. A yellow-brown glob would slide down the metal, and Tommie would shut her eyes, the bees and white heads of flowers nodding in the warm daylight and the silhouette of Gary's baseball cap written across the inside of her skull.

Her mom and her mom's boyfriend would be on the new couch watching TV, two plates greased and salted and peppered before them on the coffee table. The boyfriend—we'll call him Jessie—would turn around when Tommie opened the door with her key.

"Where've you been?"

"Jenny's."

"Your mom just called there."

"I took the long way home." Her hair falling in tangled strings about her shoulders and her skin gray in the weak light.

"It's not safe for you to be out walking around there alone in the dark, baby," her mother would call out from the couch.

"Okay."

"What do you mean okay?" Jessie would say, the girl's mother lifting her drowsy head from Jessie's lap.

"I won't do it again."

Say she stood there watching them watch the screen for a minute. Two minutes. Three. No one saying anything.

"I know someone who died watching TV."

"No you don't." Jessie turning from the screen to look at her.

"Hey, baby. Come over here and say hello." Her mother would be a little round, soft, heavy. Her hair short, all her movements slow and tired. Tired all the time. "Are you hungry?"

"Well, not someone I know," Tommie might say, coming around the couch. "Just someone I heard about. One of my teacher's dads."

"He was probably old."

"It just goes to show, you know. You die the way you live."

"Who told you that?"

"Some families do other stuff."

"Tommie, your mother is tired. She's been working her butt off for you all day. We sit here worrying about you, wondering where the hell is Tommie, and the first thing you do when you come home is tell us you don't get enough attention." Jessie might raise his voice, his neck very straight and head lifted toward her but his eyes pointed at the television.

"Give me a kiss. And go take a shower," Mom might say. "You smell like a puppy dog. Where were you all day?"

"Making mud pies."

"There isn't any mud around here," Jessie would say.

"You have everything ready for school?"

"Yep."

Then Tommie would go into the bathroom and move all her mother's and Jessie's things out of the way and fill up the tub and sneak her mother's razor to shave her legs. First time.

. . . . .

The first Monday after his father's funeral, a dark belly of heavy, low-hanging sky split open before the first line of daylight had cracked the eastern horizon. Rain splashed against the concrete and pooled in colored puddles of grease. The chilly images a forerunner of winter, an early glimpse of those dark mornings and afternoons that fill a Midwesterner's heart with dread.

Miserable in jeans and his father's ball cap nearly soaked a dark and even blue, David Lamb went in early to work, to pack up and clear out his desk. When Wilson came by in his long coat, still shaking out a cool slime of rain from his dark umbrella, Lamb sat down on the edge of his desk and faced the doorway.

"I'm sorry, David." Wilson stood in the doorway. There may have been a time when Wilson would have called him Lamb. Would have had David and Cathy over for dinner with his wife and two daughters at Wilson's house in Evanston, the kitchen full of clear, steady light glancing off the metal lake outside the French doors.

There was a time ten years earlier when he and Wilson met after work to talk about the five-year plan, the ten-year, and the twenty. Cheerfully bent on establishing their own firm, and equal partners.

They took a vacation together, then two, with their wives, with Wilson's girls.

"He was a good guy," Wilson said.

"Thanks."

Wilson held a stainless-steel mug of coffee before him like an offering, raising it a little in anticipation of stepping back and excusing himself.

"It's been one thing after another," Lamb said.

"Family in town?"

Lamb nodded. "Staying with me and Cathy."

Wilson looked down at his shoes, his ears red. "You've kind of made a mess of things here, David."

"With the girl."

"With the girl."

"She'll be all right. She just needs not having me around for a while."

"It puts me in a hell of a spot."

"I can appreciate that."

"She know you're leaving today?"

Lamb said nothing.

"Jesus, David."

"Will you give me a few weeks, Wilson? I just need a few weeks."

"She doesn't know you're divorced, either."

Lamb's face warmed. "You talked to Cathy."

"Months ago, David. July." It could not have been an easy conversation for a man like Wilson.

"There are real limits to what I can do here. This is all sort of beyond what I know how to deal with."

Lamb said nothing.

"This is a great position for Linnie, David. And she's good for us."

"I know it."

"Don't wreck her career. Take your three weeks. Take a full month, okay? Figure it out."

"I understand."

"I want you here, David. We all want you to stay. In spite of. Everything."

"Okay."

"I'll carry your accounts till we hear from you."

"I can keep them."

"No." He stepped out into the hallway. "I'll tell Karen to forward your calls. It's only a few weeks. You just go."

Leaving the office, a cardboard box under his arm, he ran into Linnie in the lobby in the long blue raincoat he bought her.

"Oh," he said. "You're in early."

Water ran from the ends of her hair. "Where are you going?"

"I'm just making calls today," he said. "Thought I'd work from home."

He looked around, lifted her chin, and kissed her lips and the corners of her mouth.

"Can you come to dinner?" She stepped back a little on one foot and looked out at the rain, sorry to be asking. "I have this really good wine."

"I know what you have." The heat rose in her face. She was a beautiful girl. Woman. He checked his watch. "I don't think I can wait for dinner."

"You say."

He lowered his voice. "Will you open your raincoat for me?"

"David. We haven't had a proper conversation in two weeks."

"We had a proper conversation last night."

Her face reddened. He loved to see it. "Come," he said and took her hand. "Let's take the stairs."

In the stairwell she twisted her hand from his. "You know there are plenty of guys who would be happy to come sample my wine."

"Lin." He kissed her mouth. "You knew how this was going to be." He kissed her neck. "Would you rather I just leave you alone?" He backed up. "This is just hurting you, isn't it?"

Nothing.

"Am I just hurting you, Lin? Am I ruining your life?" She slouched into her hips and reached her arms around his neck. He untied the belt of her raincoat. "Okay?" The coat swished in the stairwell and her shoes echoed as she adjusted her feet. They listened and watched and moved slowly. He held her head in his hand to keep it off the cinder-block wall behind her. "Right?" he said. "Is this what we do?" She nodded her head in his hand. "Say yes."

"Yes."

"Say this is what we do."

"This is what we do."

She was retying her hair when Lamb pulled her in by the loose ends of her belt and pressed his forehead to hers. Both their faces damp and warm, their breath quickened. "You should let the world have you a little more than it does," he said. "Go find your local alum chapter. Hang out with some of those young Princeton guys. Do it. Have them over for your wine. It hurts me to say, but it's the truth. You should let one of them take you to the Nine and you should share a dessert and let him put his arm around you while you walk through the city."

"Don't."

"Let me say this, Lin. It's important for me to say it. You should. You should let him walk you to the end of the pier."

"The pier is yours."

His eyes filled. "Do you mean it?"

"It's just how it is."

He looked down at his hands. "It isn't easy for me to say these things."

"I can't share myself like that David. I'm not like that."

"Oh." He let her go and leaned against the metal rail behind him. "I see."

"No, come on. I wasn't . . . I just need you to know that. It's important for me to have you know it."

"What do you want me to do with that information?"

"Just keep it for now."

"Okay. You'll tell me if there's something else I ought to do with it?"

She nodded, and again he kissed her mouth and her neck and her throat and told her she was the prettiest girl on the block, and that someday the world would be theirs and they'd have every day and every hour and every minute.

"Make your calls from here," she said, the curled fray of her bangs dry now. Her eyes big. "We can do lunch here. On the stairs."

He looked at his watch. "I'm already on my way to being late."

"Okay."

"I have a life, Lin. There are certain things I need to do."

"I know."

"Listen. I'm not stupid. I know I don't deserve you. No. I don't. And I know I'm lucky to have you now."

"Come over tonight. Please."

He went down the stairs where his box of papers and junk sat propped against the heavy door. "If you don't hear from me tonight or for a couple of days, you'll know I'm thinking of you, right? Doing the things I have to do so we can take a couple of days together."

"We should go to the Michigan dunes before it gets too cold."

"Bucket of chicken?"

"Bottle of champagne."

"Good. Pick one out. And wait for me." He opened the heavy door of the stairwell and went out.

$$\cdot \ \cdot \ \cdot \ \cdot \ \cdot$$

Two blocks from the triplet apartments Lamb found the girl, alone at her bus stop and soaked beneath a small, sagging pink umbrella.

"How did you know to come here early?" He grinned.

"How did you?" She pulled the door shut and set the umbrella at her feet. Rain dripped from her nose.

"You and me," he said. "We seem to talk without talking."

"I know. It's totally weird."

"I think maybe you were strategizing," he said. "You don't have a crush on me, do you?"

"I just like rain." Pink behind her freckles.

"I see."

"Are you driving me to school?"

"I thought we'd skip school today. Want to?"

"Duh."

"Do we need to call in? As a kindness to your worried teachers?"

"I'll just tell my mom I was sick and stayed home and she'll write me a note tomorrow."

"You've done this before?"

"Once."

He gave her a look.

"Okay, twice."

"So I'm not corrupting you."

"Nope."

"You sure?"

"Yep."

"I'm going to trust you on that." He glanced sideways at her. "Can I trust you?"

"Yes."

"Shake on it?" They shook.

He drove twenty miles west to a little town at the falls of the Fox River, where every house sat alone on a soft green hill strewn with yellow leaves. The center of town made a crooked stripe of brick and stone storefronts, of windows strung with colored glass beads or draped in damask. The sidewalks were bare and wet; no one was out. The sky was a lightless pewter and lamps inside the shops shone bright yellow. He removed his coat and put it over the girl's head and shoulders to shield her from a fine, cold rain, and he lifted his face and throat into the weather, smiling with all his teeth. He took her into a candy store and filled a little brown paper bag with Coke bottle gummies and lemon drops and sour red licorice coated with sugar. The woman behind the counter folded the bag and sealed it with a golden sticker and gave them each a vanilla buttercream. Outside he took her elbow like a gentleman, which made her laugh, and he handed over the bag.

"I would just like to draw your attention to the fact, my lady"—he cleared his throat and furrowed his brow—"that you are taking candy from a stranger."

She took the bag. "Am not."

"This is a lesson for you," he said, holding her forearm. "A man should always take your arm and let you have the inside of the walk."

"Why?"

"It's a tribute to your delicacy." He lifted their hands and twirled her in her tennis shoes. "You see?"

He walked her down two narrow flights of wooden steps stained with rainwater that ended just before a mossy falls, the wide muddy river gliding through the trees.

"Look," he said. "If you squint your eyes and plug your ears, it almost looks like an unexplored woods."

"Almost."

He stooped and held up a cold, flat stone. "Kiss it."

"The rock?"

"I'm going to make a wish on it."

She kissed the stone and he skipped it three, four, five times over the water.

"I won't even ask what you wished for."

"Smart girl." He handed her a stone. "You need a beautiful young woman to kiss it for you," he said. "But good luck finding one. I got the last one on the planet."

Say he then bought her an expensive rain jacket of her own. It was nice to buy a girl a jacket. Hers was the color of oak leaves burnt red with seven pockets and a neat little hood and pale, striped silk lining.

"It's a little grown-up," she said.

"Well. You'll grow into it." He held open the shop door, liquid music of little silver bells strung about the handle, and pulled the hood up over her head. "What will you tell your mother when she asks you where this came from?"

"I thought we were running away."

He laughed. "Don't tell her that!"

"That's not what I meant."

"I don't know," he said. "Maybe I ought to keep the jacket. Mail it to you on your seventeenth birthday. Maybe this ought to be our last outing for a while. What do you think?"

"Because it's weird?"

He looked at the girl. "Yes," he said. "Because it's weird."

She shrugged.

"Will you let me buy you a really nice hot lunch first, and we can talk it over?"

"Where?"

He pointed. Three decks up a little restaurant stacked out over the falls, its square windows bright with warmth in the drippy gloom.

The toes of their shoes were dark with rain, so Lamb asked the waitress to sit them at a table beside the lit giant stone fireplace. Once seated, Lamb raised a finger to his lips, then reached beneath the table and removed the girl's shoes, and set them on the stones before the fire.

"Gary!"

"Look," he said, turning away from the fire. "They look perfect there."

Out of heavy cloth-backed menus he ordered them both little clay bowls of buttery red soup, he ordered them both goose liver ribbon sandwiches and hot tea, and he asked her all about her mom, and Jessie, and how the days went, and did they all eat together? Never? What time did she go to bed? No bedtime? Was that a good idea? Whose idea was that? And did she wake herself in the morning or did her mom wake her? What did she eat for breakfast? Did she fix it herself? Every morning? What grocery store did they go to and what thing was she never allowed to have? Really? But that was odd. Why wouldn't her mother just buy her cashews? What was wrong with cashews? And what thing was she sick of having? Ah, he told her, Cap'n Crunch is not a meal. Burger King, he told her, did not make a family dinner. And did they spend a lot of time together on the weekends? Did they take her to the Morton Arboretum? Never? The Art Institute? The Field Museum? But that was shameful. Criminal even. And what was the biggest secret she ever kept from them? Where did Jessie keep those magazines? And how often did she look at them? And what was the worst thing she ever did? Taste booze at Sid's place? Terrible, that was terrible, what a bad kid she was after all.

"Don't become the girl who drinks too much."

"I won't."

So did he advise her, and question her, and the girl answered all of his inquiries as if Tommie were some other person in whom they were both extraordinarily interested. She became a project unto herself, split in two, adolescent-made, and he watched it happen. A sliding gray veil of rain fell outside the window behind her head. She turned around to see what he was looking at.

"Nothing," he said. "In this room your hair matches the rain."

"That figures."

"I meant it as a compliment."

"Oh."

"The polite thing to do, Tommie dear, when someone compliments you, is to just say thank you."

"Thank you."

"It makes your hair look silver." He sat very still, lowered his voice to almost whispering. "You're the silver girl. Aren't you?"

She watched him.

"I've been looking for the silver girl," he said. "And it's a shame, because when this lunch is over,

I have to put you in my truck, and take you home, and say good-bye." His thoughts washed back and forth between pitying the child and wanting to crush her, stamp her out for her own sake. Because he knew exactly what the rest of her life would be after he returned her, and it was a bleak and terrible secret that he and all the world were keeping from her, and his withholding was the worst of all, because his presence in her life—this sudden and unusual friendship—might be the only bright spot, the only break in an otherwise scripted life. She was an arm's length away. He could reach her, he could show her something else, just briefly, just for a page of her life. She was just close enough to warn. With a small bright spoon she ate from her glass dish of crème fraîche and the last of summer's crushed blackberries.

He leaned in close over the tabletop, moved the crystal salt and pepper shakers aside, beckoned her closer with his forefinger.

"You know what, Tom? I'd rather sit here all day with you and order you dinner at eight than do anything else in the world."

"What would we have?"

"Roast duck. Wild rice. Baby carrots in butter. Warm bread and mushroom soup and baked apples. We'd sit here until the rain turned to snow and filled up the streets, and all the waiters and waitresses went home. Till the snow filled up the windows and the whole room turned blue, and the fire went out, and I'd make you a little nest of these beautiful red tablecloths and tuck you in."

And there was nothing wrong with all that, was there? With a guy like him buying a kid like her a nice lunch, spoiling her a little? It was good for her. It was just a little tonic for his poisonous heart. Right? Why shouldn't he have that? It was good for them both. And so it was good for everybody— because that's how goodness works. It spills like water, bleeds into everyone, into everything, into trees, rivers, cracks in sidewalks. And Christ, it gave him such a feeling to put that nice new coat on her, to button it up right beneath her freckled chin.

It was just a day with a girl, right? Just a couple of harmless days, and he'd leave her alone by and by. He would become the source of a few odd treasures in the wreck of her bedroom closet. She'd forget all about him by Christmas. But when they were back in the truck driving east, back into the filth of the city, as if without warning from himself, he slowed down and looked sideways at her.

"What?"

"You really want to see the mountains?"

"Duh."

"You want to go with me? A week?"

"Where?"

"I'm not just talking here. I mean it. It might be risky. You might get in trouble when you get back."

"A week?"

"Just a little secret trip in your secret life. You'll get your camping trip. Something to keep in your pocket when you're back in this place and forty years old and I'm dead and buried. Right? Like the pencil sharpener? We could eat at little restaurants like that one, and drive way out across the country, and survey the grounds, then turn around and bring you home? What do you say?"

"Yeah."

"And I'll spoil you up. And you'll never tell anyone where we went? Swear to God?"

"Swear to God."

"Not even your mom?"

"Not even my mom."

"Not even Sid."

"No way."

"You have to swear."

"I swear."

"Not even your husband in forty years when I've been dead for practically forever?"

"Okay."

"Cross your heart."

She crossed her flat chest. "Hope to die."

"Want to leave now?"

"I don't have my stuff."

"I'll get you stuff."

"You will?"

"All the useful things you'll need. We can make a list of supplies, right?"

"What about my mom and Jessie?"

"We'll have to talk about that."

"I don't think we should ask."

"Neither do I."

"Because they'd never let me. Maybe mom. But Jessie, never."

"I'll bring you back before anyone gets too worried. One week? Monday through Sunday. You won't be gone two Mondays. Six days. Five nights."

The girl made a crazy face, as if to say: this is crazy. As if to say: yeah.

"Did you ever stay away from home for a week?"

"Five days."

"An uncle's?"

"Grandma's."

"Out of state?"

"Michigan."

"Detroit?"

"Holland."

"Okay. Is this like going to Grandma's in Holland?"

"Sort of. Not really."

He frowned. "What if we get halfway there and you want to turn around?"

"I won't."

"Promise?"

"Promise."

"I'm going to do everything in my power to make you want to keep going."

"Ooo. I'm scared."

"I'm just letting you know. I'm a really smart guy."

"Says who?"

"I do. I get to say. And you better get used to it."

"Why?"

"Because," he said, "I have all the money."

"Oh, yeah."

. . . . .

So you see, none of this was planned. This is the kind of unforeseeable map that arises one bright little city at a time. It's about letting go of the clench in your forehead and letting your heart steer. And it isn't as easy as it sounds.

In the hotel lobby, everything was white. The floor of bleached ceramic tiles; the high frosted ceiling supported by smooth, ash-colored marble columns. Tommie stared around as if she'd been transported to another world.

"Are you afraid?" he asked in the elevator.

"No."

They rushed silently upward.

"Are you being honest?"

"I've never been anywhere like this."

"I know."

"Are you really rich?"

The doors opened.

"Now listen," he said as he walked her down the corridor. She pushed the hair out of her face. Like a little woman. "This is just an intermediary step, right? This trip is not for certain. We're going to do this in stages." He unlocked the door with the plastic card and held it open for her. "And maybe not at all."

The room was warm and dry and smelled of citrus and balsam and clean linen. The creamy whites of the down comforters and painted walls were softly lit. Outside the giant panes of glass the dark sky was lifting and cracking apart. Lamb and the girl stood together near the door a moment, as if the room were intended for some other couple.

"Do you want the bed by the window or by the bathroom?"

"Duh, window." She went in.

"Good."

He opened the armoire and turned on the television, searching the channels. "What do you like? You like cartoons?"

She rolled her eyes. "Please."

He tossed her the remote and rezipped his jacket.

"Are we going someplace?"

"I am. To get supplies."

"For the road?"

"Yes," he said. "For the road."

"How long will it take to get there?"

"Two days."

"How can we make it back in five nights?"

He looked down at his hands, then moved his mouth as he counted in his head. "This is exactly why we're doing this in stages," he said. "So we don't do anything stupid. It might actually be seven nights. Or ten."

"Can't I come with you now?"

"No."

"Why?"

"Three reasons. First, because it's warm in here. And we don't want you getting sick. Second, I want you to be alone for an hour or so. You know how to get home from here, more or less?"

She gave him a blank look, so he opened a drawer in the little white desk and took out the binder of guest information. "Here." He put four twenties on the desk. "That's for a cab home. And a little extra."

"I don't want to go home."

"I want you to think about it. I want you to take this hour and think real hard about whether or not you should stay and wait for me. This will look a lot to other people like I'm kidnapping you. Right?"

"Oh."

"It will. I'm fifty-four years old, and you?"

"Eleven."

He inhaled. Christ. He'd taken her for thirteen at least. Eleven. That was closer to five years old than it was to eighteen. Her friends did not look eleven. The blond one—she could've been sixteen. He looked at his hands. At the floor. He did not look at her when he gave her the last reason.

"And three, here you are," he said, "alone in a hotel room with a stranger. And eleven."

"But you're not a stranger."

"Well. Maybe you feel a little funny."

"I don't feel funny."

"Maybe you're just not letting yourself feel funny. Think about all the ways this situation could make a girl your age feel. Okay? Say okay, Gary."

"Okay, Gary."

"And then, if you choose to stay, I want you to make this room yours. Do some rearranging. Put your shoes over there, and wash your face, and mess up the pillows. Make it like it's your own room. So when I come back, it'll be like you're inviting me into your room, okay?"

"You're weird."

"Maybe so. But I know what I'm talking about. And if you don't want me to come in when I get back, you can hand me my stuff and I'll go get another room. Right?" He'd meant to sound forceful, convincing, but he was almost whispering.

"That won't happen."

"Just say okay, Gary."

"Okay, Gary."

"And if I come back and you're gone, I'll understand you've gone home. And no hard feelings, okay? It wouldn't mean we can't—you know—hang out. Like before. Say it: no hard feelings."

"No hard feelings."

"Good. Good girl." He squinted at her. "Are all seventh graders eleven? I mean, your friends look a little old for their age."

She shrugged. "I'll be twelve in December."

He looked down at the floor and nodded.

"Can I ask you a question?"

He sat on the edge of the other bed.

"What if I want to come home? Not like I will."

"I'll put you on a plane. Straight home, first class."

"Okay."

"And I'll buy you a little purse, and fill it with money and snacks and a magazine or comic book. And I'll send you on your way."

"Okay."

"It'll be an open door, all the time. If you decide you can't bear the drive back with me, if you decide I'm just like some mean old uncle, too strict, or if I preach too much, I'll buy you the plane ticket. I give you my word."

"Okay."

"It'll be just like vacation, so you can see some other things. Something other than this sad place."

She nodded.

"You're not like your friends, are you?"

"I don't know."

"You're not," he said. "You believe that?"

"If you say so."

He grinned. "That's my girl. So we have a deal?" He turned over his palm and spat in it, and extended his hand. She snorted, and grinned, and spat in her own hand, and they shook.

Lamb left her in the white hotel and drove back toward the city, away from the last broken reaches of daylight as rain clouds threaded with neon blue in the rearview mirror. The girl would be there when he returned. Not because she wanted to go but because she wouldn't take the initiative to call a cab.

He turned into the parking lot of Tommie's building and pulled up to the front. There was a different

security guard—a heavy young guy in cheap black
pants and a windbreaker with the same corporate
logo on the breast. Already balding and pale and
bereft of all those heartbreaking nights a young guy
like him should be suffering. A young guy only has
so many nights in him during his tenure on planet
Earth, and he ought not squander them alone in ruined parking lots, bothering people. He came right
up to the driver's side of the truck.

"You looking for somebody, man?"

Lamb's pulse raced up his neck and down his
arms, the taste of his own breath foul in his mouth.
"Is this Roosevelt Road?" He pointed at the six-
lane. "I seem to have gotten turned around."

The man shook his head. "No, man."

"I need to go west?"

"You can't make a left turn here." A small, round
woman with chin-length grayish-brown hair tilted
sideways a little beneath the weight of a huge canvas satchel swung over her shoulder. Lamb watched
her walk by as the man gave him directions he didn't
need, and he became very, very still.

Perhaps it was in this moment that Lamb made up
his mind, when he came right up against the emp-
tiness. And who's to blame him if he then turned
completely—shoulders, face, hands, pelvis—to the
girl? She pulled him back into himself and into a concrete world that, frankly, David Lamb wasn't quite

ready to surrender. He wasn't ready to surrender the story he thought he was in. Not in the way this parking lot and this pasty thin-haired man had just somehow rendered not only possible but necessary.

Lamb wanted the greasy cars and the soft white bed at the hotel; he wanted to stuff ice cream and roast turkey down the girl's tiny gullet until she puked laughing; he wanted the pain of seeing Cathy on the arm of some other man, some gentle-hearted egghead in a fleece jacket and with a beautiful red dog because she deserved those things; he wanted cold fingers and hot coffee and fried eggs and he wanted Linnie's wine and he wanted Linnie again, her body pressed into his and the envy of men's faces when he entered a room with her; he wanted snow disappearing into the cold pewter spill of Lake Michigan in December and he wanted headaches and sleepless nights and waking up knowing he had a heart because it was spinning in a mechanical whir behind his ribs. And he wanted all of these things twice: he wanted them, and he wanted knowing he was getting them.

He rolled up the window against the security guard and took a left-hand turn out of the lot, sped down the street and onto 90 and into the city. He called Linnie from outside her narrow brick town house, and in less than a minute she was standing inside the gold-lit doorway in a sweater and her wonderful blue jeans, her dark hair all around her.

"I can't stay long."

"I know."

"I'm heading out of town for a bit, Lin."

"To the cabin?"

"Tomorrow. For a few weeks."

"Am I invited?" She took his coat. "Come sit. Wine?"

"Please, Lin. You're invited everywhere. Can we fly you out? Over the weekend? Will you come?"

"Of course." She set two glasses on her tiny kitchen table.

"I knew you would," he said, and leaned back, and looked up at her.

"Of course you did."

Ninety minutes later at the Residence Inn, Lamb unmade his bed, packed his belongings, ordered room service, and called Draper, who he knew was loaded down for the month, and invited him to dinner.

"Can't do it, Davy. Next week?"

"Good. Next week. Call me when you're freed up?"

And he called Draper's wife. Left her a message. Invited her out to the cabin too. He ate half the salad and half the halibut and set the tray on the floor by the door. Then he loaded up the truck and left the hotel.

At a deserted Kmart halfway back to the white hotel he packed up for the road. Warm clothes for the girl, bottled water, bubblegum, potato chips, soda, paper cups, apple juice, crackers, Slim Jims, Oreos, a bag of apples. He put a quarter in a junk machine and turned the metal key and pocketed a small plastic ring in a big plastic bubble.

When he stood at last before the door to their room, he took a single long breath, ran his hand through his hair, and checked his fly. He knocked before walking in.

There she was, the white down blanket pulled over her head like a cape. Like she was a little old lady, a thousand years old, propped up on a mound of six or seven giant pillows. She gave him a silly grin. "This bed is awesome."

"What are you doing?"

"Just sitting here."

"No TV?" He carried the plastic bag of clothes to the foot of her bed.

"Just imagining things."

"What things?"

"You know. How you imagine you're different than in real life. Like you have longer hair. Or you're smarter. Something like that."

"And you're still here," he said.

"Ta-da."

"Are you the best girl in the world, or what?"

She scrunched up her face.

"I bought you a sweater," he said, "and some blue jeans."

"You did?"

"I'm going to make you a deal. Every time the temperature drops ten degrees, I'll buy you a new sweater."

"Will it be cold?"

"At night and early morning." He opened the bag and took her things out. "I'm sorry they're from Kmart. We'll get you nice things when we have more time."

"Are we in a rush?"

"We just want to make good time, right?"

She nodded and took the sweater from him and put it against her cheek. "It's soft."

"It's a good color for you."

"My mom says it's not."

"Well, moms don't know everything." He took out the jeans and removed all the plastic tags and set it all up for her at the desk. "For the morning."

"Thanks."

"You hungry?"

"Nope."

"You ready to hit the sack?"

"Sure."

"You want a bedtime story?"

"I'm not six."

"I know how old you are. Who doesn't like a bedtime story?"

"I'm too old."

"Well, I'm going to help you get over that. You're lucky you found me. I'm going to keep you on the straight and narrow."

"Sounds boring."

"That's what everybody thinks. Now come on. Did you wash your face?"

"Yes."

"With soap?"

They both looked at the bathroom counter where the hotel soap was stacked in a pile of three shiny paper squares. The girl groaned and stood up. "What are you, my dad or something?"

"That's a good way to think of it. That's exactly how I want you to think about it."

. . . . .

They would have been on the east-west tollway, bright white farm-field daylight, when Lamb sped past the last county sign for Rock Island, Illinois. The girl sat beside him in her new yellow sweater, watching the road as if the reels of flat highway needling fast and straight ahead were the opening credits of some film she was either bound to watch or in which she had just willingly agreed to perform.

They'd left the hotel in the dark, didn't stop for breakfast until a rest stop past Aurora. And because she was his lookout, his sidekick in the passenger seat, he bought her a syrupy hot chocolate from a machine and made a little wide-eyed show of adding extra packets of sugar. The lookout, he said, stirring the cocoa, has to keep her wits about her, has to be alert, must be the eyes and ears.

"Unless," he said, starting the truck, "you want to turn around and go back home now?"

"Nope."

"You'll tell me when?"

"Okay, but I won't want to."

"I'm serious. You tell me when."

"I will."

Down the road they tapped their cups together at the hour when school would have started, and she wanted to toast again when she figured Sid and Jenny were being questioned for the first time.

"Were they so very awful?" he asked her.

She nodded.

"What was the worst thing they did."

She turned and stared out the window. "What they said."

"What did they say?"

"The worst?"

"The worst."

"They pretended like no one else was in the room and had this really loud talk while we waited for the teacher. Sid said it was no surprise that I hooked up with you. And Jenny said I must be used to it since my stepdad makes little visits to my room every night. And, you know, everybody was looking at me."

"Did you leave the room?"

"He's not even my stepdad. They're not even married."

"You stayed. Did you cry?"

"No."

He glanced at her. "Is it true about Jessie?"

"No. He takes me swimming in the morning and they make this big thing out of it."

"I see."

"I guess it doesn't sound as bad as it really was."

"No," he said. "It sounds pretty bad."

The girl turned to him. "Gary?"

"Yes, ma'am."

"Why didn't you ever get married?"

"I suppose I never found the right girl."

"Oh."

"Did you ever have a boyfriend? Like Jenny and Sidney?"

She shrugged and looked out the window. "Not like that. Not serious."

"What's serious? Like you weren't in love?"

"Not hooking up or anything."

"Hooking up."

"Like messing around."

"You never?"

She rolled her eyes.

"What is that?" Lamb said. "Like it's no big deal?"

She shrugged.

He slowed down. "I don't like that, Tommie." He steered the truck onto the shoulder and put it in park.

"What are we doing?"

"I'm going to tell you something really important," he said. "Are you listening?" He reached into his front pocket and pulled out a handful of coins. He sorted them, and held up a penny. He turned it over in his hand. "What year were you born?"

"Nineteen ninety-six."

"I was forty-four years old."

"Whoa."

"Don't say that. Don't say whoa. Makes me feel like I should take you back home."

She slid her hands beneath her bottom and tipped her head. "What were you doing back then?"

LAMB

He stopped turning the penny and looked at her.

"I might tell you sometime," he said, as if he were surprised to be saying it.

"Okay."

"Do you know how much a stamp costs?"

"Like fifty cents?"

"In nineteen fifty-two, Tommie, a first-class stamp cost a man three cents."

"Whoa."

"In nineteen fifty-two, Tommie, the United States federal government spent about sixty-eight billion dollars. Total." He looked at her. "That doesn't mean anything to you, does it?"

"Not really."

"We need to do a better job learning about the world around us."

"Don't do that. Jessie does that."

"Does what?"

"Says we when you mean me."

He put his hands in his lap. "You're right."

She shrugged.

"Shrug it off. Get real good at shrugging. That girl? She's a shrugger. Nothing gets to her."

She looked at him sideways and rolled her eyes.

"It hurts my feelings that you shrug and roll your eyes. That you talk like you're already grown up. That you don't know about nineteen fifty-two. I'm

71

trying to help you here, I'm trying to tell you something important."

"Sorry."

"Christ, the people your age. There isn't a wild place left on the planet for you. There isn't a code of decency or manners left for you to break. And what do you do? You shrug." He took her hand and turned it over and pressed the penny into it. "Your piece of the year I was born. Don't lose it. That might be all you get."

She looked at the penny in her hand. "I'm sorry."

"Someday," he said, "we'll rent a trailer. A silver one. Just like it was fifty years ago. And you'll be seventeen and we'll put you in a long skirt and tie your hair back with a dotted yellow scarf and drive across the country, from ice cream stand to ice cream stand. We'll map it out just right, so that every city we hit is in the peak of springtime, cool wind and green puddles and white blossoms and all of that. Bright sun and rain shaking out of the trees and new birds and you and your yellow scarf."

"Will you pick me up at school?"

"In the silver trailer."

"Deal."

"Listen, Tom. Can I ask you a serious question?"

"What."

"Yes or no."

"Yes."

"You haven't hooked up with a boy, have you?" Her skin went pink behind her freckles. "You maybe lied to Sid or Jenny and said you did, but you never really did, did you?" She shook her head. "Because it's a very big deal," he said. "The biggest deal. And listen. I want you to hear me. In case you're having funny thoughts. I am not going to kiss you. It's my way of honoring you. Do you understand? It's my way of honoring nineteen fifty-two. And the little cabin out there. And the river."

"That's all real?"

"What do you mean?"

"The cabin and the river?"

"Isn't that where we're going?"

"I mean the shop with the pickle jar. The horse. That's all pretend."

"It's all real, Tommie."

"For real for real?"

"I'm not a liar."

"Me either."

"Good. I know you're not. You sometimes talk silly, but you're basically a pretty good girl, aren't you?"

"Yeah."

"I know," he said. "Hey, where's that penny?"

She opened her hand and he took the coin, put it on the end of his thumb, and pressed it to the center of her forehead.

"Ouch."

"Ssh." He pressed hard. "There," he said, "the year I was born, printed right on your beautiful freckled forehead."

She touched it but couldn't make it out.

"Can you feel it?"

"Yes."

"Heads or tails?"

She felt again. "Heads."

"It's tails." He grinned. "Know what that means?"

"It means you win."

"No," he said. "Don't think of it that way." Beside the truck a semi hurtled past, then another. "I'll tell you what it means. It means you're my good luck."

She smiled.

"I sort of knew it the minute I saw you."

"You did?"

He rolled down the windows. "Stick your hand out there, will you?" Sunlight flashed on her little gold ring with the fake pink stone. "Memorize that," he said. "There will be days when you're back in Chicago, all grown up, lines in your face, and there will be no tall grass and be no birdsong and no wide-open road and you'll wish you were back here. You'll wonder what ever happened to that one old guy who drove you around that one September."

The road was still. No cars, nothing but the highway and the bright sky and the fat sun. No witness but the hushed and high green corn.

"Gary," she said. "I know it's not just for a week."

He looked at her.

"I know you had to say just a week or we never would have left."

"Don't say that," he whispered. "It isn't true." He stared at her, his face suddenly very warm.

She stared back at him.

"Is this a bad idea?" His voice was clear and careful in the new quiet. "I think this might be a really bad idea. I think maybe we better turn around." He picked up Tommie's hand. "Listen," he said. "I want you to think about how this looks. You're in middle school. You're smart. You know some things. You've seen the news, right? Say right."

"Right."

"Good. So I want you to imagine you're that truck driver." He nodded at the windshield. "And you stopped the truck because sometimes with a load like that, the spools can rock and come unhitched. And you're a really careful driver, and you check every two hundred miles."

"Okay."

"And you're walking around to the back of your load, and you're thinking about the lemon iced tea and chicken salad sandwich you'll have at the Jette Diner in Iowa City. And you're thinking a little bit about your little boy in South Bend—that's in Indiana. You hope he's doing his math homework, and you're adjusting the ball cap on your head, when you see us. You see me, and you see yourself, a man and a girl just like we are, in a truck like this, and the man is holding the girl's hand, just like this, and talking to her very earnestly, just like we are. What would you think? Tell me. And don't spare me."

Tommie considered, tipped her head sideways and lifted her chin. "Well. I guess I'd think some guy and his kid."

"A guy and his kid. Like his granddaughter?"

"Yeah. No. Like his daughter."

He nodded. "And if somebody asked you, you could look them in the eye and say that's what we are?"

"Sure."

"Let's practice." He let go her hand. "Hey, kid, who's that guy you're with?"

Tommie straightened her neck, looked off into the middle distance. "What guy? Him? You mean my dad?"

They both laughed. "You're good," he said. "You're very good. You could be an actress."

76

"Thank you."

"It wasn't a compliment," he said. "Hey. We could be a guy and a girl pretending to be an actor and an actress. How about that?"

She scrunched up her nose. "You're confusing me."

"You make it so easy to do." He laughed and she crossed her arms but she was grinning. "And you're sure you want to drive all the way through Iowa with me? And into Nebraska and Colorado and all the way out to that great ridge of rock?"

"Yeah."

"And I'm not kidnapping you. And I don't want to hug you or kiss you or be, you know, that way."

"I know."

"Good. So we're really on?"

"On."

"I'm serious, Tom."

"Me too."

"Then Rocky Mountains, here we come." He extended his hand, and again, they shook.

While the girl was in the bathroom at a Chevron in a travel stop off I-80, Lamb bought two postcards and walked outside to the edge of the broken asphalt where trash and weeds grew in a ragged line and broken glass glittered. It was hot, and everything looked new, lighter, open. He was cut loose from the world, off the screen. He lifted his face into the heat, turned on his phone and checked for messages as he watched the front of the Chevron. He stepped over a flattened silver can, its label bleached by sunlight. A plastic straw. A yellow paper burger wrapper. He dialed Linnie.

"I got your message. I'm sorry I missed you." The sun was high and it seared off the windshields and mirrors of cars in the filling station lot. A man in a blue jumpsuit was hosing down the lot beside a gas pump and the water sprayed like liquid light. "Are you set to go? Let me know if you're coming." Tommie stepped out, shielding her eyes with her hand and looking for him. "I want you to picture me thinking of you, Linnie. That's how it will be. Call me. I have my cell. It'll be on when I'm not out of range."

He shut the phone as the girl approached him. "Who you talking to?"

"One of my many bosses."

"Are you in trouble?"

"No. Why? Are you?"

. . . . .

Just outside of West Des Moines, set back among the ash and oak and a dozen miles off the interstate, no neighbors but a filling station and a mom-and-pop burger joint where they cut the french fries themselves, there's a little motel spread out in fourteen tiny green cabins like game pieces on a sloping grassy board. The parking lot is breaking apart, gradually elevated by a plain of grass rising up beneath it, lifting and bearing the asphalt away as a giant sea drains off the edges of a newborn world. Each cabin is neat and newly painted. Behind the desk in the little office, they rent you rolled-up bath towels and sell nickel bars of white soap. It is as though the hands of all the Midwestern clocks had done nothing for fifty years but spin on battery-powered bolts.

"This is the world's most perfect motel." Lamb drove the Ford onto the uneven lot. "Now we know we're on our way."

There were twin beds in cabin number four. The girl sat on one of them and kicked off her filthy Keds.

"You need some new shoes."

"I know. My toes are popping out."

"Didn't your mother take you shopping for school shoes?"

"Not yet."

"Let's put it on the list of necessary supplies. Make a mental note."

"Okay." She leaned back into the pillows. "I'm pooped."

"Aren't you going to let me turn down the bed for you?"

"Turn down the bed?"

"You're the kind of girl," he said, walking between the beds, "who ought to have some poor old guy turn down the bed for you every night of your life." She laughed, but he was very solemn and waited for her to stand. He lifted the pillow and folded the heavy striped bedspread down to the footboard, then turned back the corner of the white sheets and bright blue woolen blanket into a neat triangle.

"This is like my grandma's."

"Michigan?"

"Yes."

"That's where your mom is from?"

"Yep."

"Are you missing home?"

"No. A little."

"That's good," he said. "If we're going to be partners, we have to be square with each other, right?"

"Sure."

He hit his forehead with the heel of his hand. "Boy am I stupid."

"What?"

"Pajamas. We forgot to get you pajamas. A girl can't sleep in her blue jeans."

"I slept in my clothes at the other hotel."

"And you shouldn't have. It was an inexcusable oversight, starting our trip that way."

She put her hands on her jeans. "But these are brand-new. Spanking clean."

"Spanking clean?"

"Yes."

He shook his head. "I'll step outside and wait two minutes, okay? I'll count to sixty twice. Very slowly. I'll honor each number fully: thirty-two, thirty-three—just like that. You take off your slacks and fold them on the back of the desk chair, and scrub your face in the sink. Use a washcloth. And soap. Then in bed. In the morning we'll do it all backwards."

"Slacks?"

"Look," he said, "give me a break?"

She heard him outside the door counting. Sixty, fifty-nine, fifty-eight. And she did everything just as he said, washed her face with the little rectangle of perfumed soap, thirty-six, thirty-five, and a thin white washcloth, and combed her hair with her fingers, twenty-one, twenty, and checked her profile in the mirror this way, then that, and pulled back her T-shirt tight and checked for breasts, then got undressed, nine, eight, and stretched out her legs under the cold white sheets.

When Lamb stepped back into the room, he stopped short. He walked between the beds and reached for a lamp switch shaped like a small brass key. He looked at the girl's jeans and T-shirt on the floor.

"There are your clothes."

He bent over and retrieved them, one piece at a time, folded them, and placed them over the back of the chair, and gave her a look with his eyebrows arched.

"Got it."

"You look so clean and fresh," he said. "Belly full of pizza. Happy, yes?"

She nodded.

"Good," he said. "That's my job. Keep you happy. And you can help by telling me when you're not. Or when you think you might not be. Right?"

"This is the life."

"You're sweet." He picked up a paper sack and withdrew two plastic cups, one purple and one green, with cartoon characters dancing around the rim. "It's all they had."

"SpongeBob."

"If you say so."

He took out a red cardboard quart of whole milk and filled the cups, then took the pillow off his own bed and propped her up, touching her shoulders and the back of her head. Arranging her just so. Then he put one plastic cup of milk in her hand.

"Let me see you drink that," he said. "God, you look good. You look just like the perfect . . . little person. Go on. It's good for you."

She smiled at him.

"Don't you like milk?" he asked, alarmed.

"Sure."

"But you think I'm treating you like a baby, don't you? I'm not. A young woman like yourself needs milk for her bones."

He raised his cup and she hers. They drank.

"I was really smart to get that milk." He grinned. "It was just what you needed in that twin bed."

She leaned back into the pillows and looked at him over the rim of the little cup, where he sat on the edge of his own bed.

"This is a good moment. Far from the city. In our neat little twin beds and the clean night air outside the window. It's like camping. Or like we're brother and sister, sharing a room."

She snorted. "You're the big brother, I guess."

"No, I'm not. I'm the little brother. You're the big sister. The tall one. The smart one. Right? And you'll help me learn all the things about the world that I need to know."

"Gary."

"Yes, dear."

"I think I maybe want to call my mom."

"Okay."

"Okay?"

"In the morning?"

"Sure."

"What do you want to tell her?"

"Just that everything is okay, and I'm okay, and don't worry."

"Do you think she'll probably worry anyway?"

"Yeah."

"Do you think a phone call might make her worry more?"

"I don't know."

"Maybe we should think about that."

He took the cup from her hands and set it on the nightstand and turned out the lights. He shifted his heavy body to his own bed, his head piled up in his arms, his voice a soft static.

"You know that old horse I was telling you about?" Her hair rustled against the pillows. "In this story, he's red. Do you want to hear it?"

"Sure."

"When our girl, the one in this story, found him, he was on the one thousand and eleventh floor of a tall glass building, in a cold and crowded city. All the people in the building had small glass offices, and everything was covered in mirrors. The ceilings were mirrors, the walls too. Every man in a pale shirt and a dark tie and every woman in a straight blue pencil skirt and each of them casting a trillion reflections of themselves deep into the walls and floors and ceilings about them. Can you picture that?"

"Mmm."

She watched him talking, leaning sideways on the bed, propped up on one elbow, one boot stacked upon the other.

"It made the red horse dizzy and our girl could tell. He was stuck up there, staring down the long fractured silver hallway. Our girl was in a yellow dress, just exactly the color of fresh butter, and she led the red horse toward the mirror-faced elevator and rode him into the car and down they went. Down ten floors and her heart rose up in her chest and the pelt of the warm horse lifted against the palm of her hand and down faster, faster they went. Are you listening?"

"I'm sleepy."

"Good. Down ten more floors. A hundred. Down, down, down. Her heart rising up into her throat from the speed of it. Her head pounding like birds' wings and her limbs were heavy, heavier and heavier. Suddenly the doors opened on the seventy-seventh floor. Trillions of reflections, arms filled with papers and green file folders, and they all stared at the girl and the horse, but then the elevator doors winked shut and the car hurtled down again, the girl's butter-colored dress rising up to her knees and up to her hips and up over her head and then suddenly it was over. The doors opened, and they stepped out."

"Thank God," the girl murmured from her sleep.

He laughed. "Yes. That's right. But outside on the street was even worse. Steel cars and concrete and noise and the girl leaned over the horse and she promised to get him home. You don't belong here, she whispered to him. And neither do I. Are you awake?"

"Sort of."

"She led him between the rows of black and blue cars and out of the city. They rested behind a gas station, slept on the flat, hard dirt glittering with bits of broken glass and shreds of gum wrappers and foil. By the time they reached Iowa, they were both sleepy and famished."

"They were so tired."

"Yes. They were." He reached across the space between them and pinched her arm. She yelped. He was surprised by how much it quickened him to do it. "Stay awake," he said. "We're almost there. The sun was going down in Iowa. Everything looked so soft. Stems of tall weedy flowers bending this way and that, the grass was green and leaves on the bur oaks were green, all of it darkening, green to blue to black as the sun went down. Shadows of narrow tree trunks fell across the ground, and way, way off the highway was a tiny house with square windows yellow in the growing dark. The girl slipped down off the horse's soft damp back. Her yellow dress was dirty, her arms and cheeks sunburnt. The horse followed her through the high wet grass toward the house. She turned back to see that he was following, and he nuzzled her beneath the chin."

"Hey." The girl suddenly sat up a little. "What kind of messed-up story is this?"

"What? Messed up?" Lamb made a face like he'd been wounded and he held his hands over his heart. "Where would you get such an idea?"

"I don't know."

"Well, I do. And out on the Old El Rancho Road there will be no TV. None."

"I like TV."

"No you don't. You just think you do."

"That's not true."

"Did you ever live in a house without one?"

"No."

"Then what makes you think it wouldn't be better?"

She was silent.

"Listen, Tommie. It's a beautiful story, okay? It isn't messed up at all. If you're expecting it to be, I'll just stop now. Maybe you don't want to hear it."

"Yes, I do."

"Good. Are you comfortable?"

"Yes."

"And you want to know what happens next?"

"Just tell it."

"Our girl went up to the windows and looked into the dark kitchen. The horse helped her in over the sill. When she came out she was carrying a bag of soft white bread, and she and the horse crossed the field again, lumbering, crossed the highway, and settled beneath a maple tree all black and blue in the twilight. The girl leaned her body against the horse. He was warm. She opened the bag and one soft white pillow at a time fed herself, and then the horse, both of them chewing, happy because they'd escaped, but heavy and slow because they were so, so tired. The horse could hardly keep his beautiful red face up, and the girl could scarcely keep lifting the bread to his mouth. A breeze pulled the ends of her hair and all the trees turned into night trees. And there they slept, so soundly that the whole night passed in a single perfect moment."

Tommie started out of sleep. "I still have both pillows."

"I know." He smiled. "You looked so good sleeping on them. You looked just like a sleepy freckled pig. I was watching you. I was watching your round belly rising under the blankets, and watching you hog all the pillows. You were snoring!"

"I wasn't even asleep."

"You were."

"I'm sorry. Here." She pushed one of the pillows at him, and the other. "Have both."

"Uh-oh. She wanted to turn him into a pig too. But he wasn't having any of that. Besides"—he pointed at the green curtains drawn across the little frame window—"it'll be daylight soon. We got to get out and catch the morning. I'll step outside while you get dressed." He was up on his feet.

"Did we sleep?"

"What a question."

"You slept with your boots on."

"I guess I did."

"What time is it?"

"Don't you worry about the time. Don't you worry about a thing, little miss piggy. I'll watch the calendar for us both, okay? The Mondays and the Tuedays and the Wednesdays." He looked at her bare arms and shoulders above the polyester edging on the wool blanket, then opened the door and stepped out into the dark.

. . . . .

Let's say there were none of those truss towers of galvanized steel lining the highway this next day. No telephone poles. No wires. Say that Lamb's truck and the highway were the only relics of the actual world. The road was overcome with native grasses and aromatic flowers, with wild onion and pussytoes. Soft gaping mouths of beardtongue, and mountain lover, and buckbush and drowsy purple heads of virgin's bower. Say it was like this that they crossed the Midwestern line beyond which the sky spreads itself open—suddenly boundless, suddenly an awful blue.

Tommie sat cross-legged in the passenger seat and Lamb glanced sideways thinking that if she were in fact to break away from the truck, somehow, he would let her go.

"What're you thinking about over there?"

"Nothing." Outside her window was the roofless shell of a pine board homestead. She had her shoulders hiked up, her little mouth open, a crease between her brows.

"Sort of beautiful the way it's all destroyed."

"I know."

"You sound smarter every time you agree with me." He winked, stopping the car on the shoulder. "We're in Wyoming now. Were you wondering? You can always just ask and I'll tell you exactly where we are."

"Okay."

"That out there." He pointed to the little ruin of sloping, black-mouthed house. "That could have been the first homestead in the Wyoming Territory.

Maybe eighteen fifty. That little broken home could be Cheyenne. First mark on a fresh and hairy green plain."

"It's yellow."

"You can imagine it green."

She looked out the window.

"You want to go see?"

She shrugged.

"I know," he said. "It's farther than it looks and you're tired." He raised his voice a bit. "It was a once-in-a-lifetime journey back in time. But our girl was sleepy."

"Okay. Let's get out."

He raised his fingertips to his ear.

"Yes!" she said. "Open the door!"

"That's exactly how I want to hear it. I'm just your guide, right? This is your trip. This is your week. I'll have this cabin for the rest of my life. I'll have this highway. But this is the only time you'll get to see it. So come on. Let me hear it: It's my week, Gary."

"It's my week, Gary."

"Good. I want you to be greedy about it." He unlocked the doors.

They went over the gravel shoulder and down the irrigation ditch and up again onto hard dry ground. To the north, scores of slanted wooden snow fences set in the grass like empty easels. The wind was loud and the sagebrush shook like knotted gray fists. As far east and as far west as the eye could see, wood posts and a three-wire fence. A blue plastic bag turned over itself in the grass.

"Oh," she said. "We can't."

"Oh, you sweet little thing." He lifted one of the wires between its barbs and held it open. "That's just a fence."

She stepped through and he followed.

"Ready?" he said, brushing his hands on the thighs of his blue jeans. "Set. Go!" He took off running, his black-and-silver head flashing in the dazzle. "Try to keep up, you lazy pillow pig!" She ran after him and he grinned back at her puffing and bobbing over the uneven ground, stopping her with an arm across her belly when she approached the house. The tops of her cheeks were pink behind her freckles, and her hair stuck in sweat to her temples.

"Careful," he said. Rusted orange nails pointed up from the overturned boards.

Glassless windows, all the house wood gray. A rocking chair the color of dirt sat oddly intact and perfectly still on the wood-slab porch.

"Someone must have brought it out," he said, looking at it. "You see any beer cans, you'll know for sure."

"Kids come here?"

"I bet some guy dragged a mattress out here in his old man's truck and hauled out a bunch of flashlights and cheap wine and paper cups and cigarettes, and brings out a different girl every Saturday night."

"Gary!"

He put his hands up in the wind. "Hey, I'm just a guy telling you how it is. It's better if you know. Consider yourself warned."

"Sick."

"Do you want to go inside and see?"

"No. It gives me a spooky feeling."

"I know," he said.

"Do you think they died here?"

"Who? The girlfriends?"

"No, dummy." She punched him lightly in the arm and pulled down on her T-shirt, lifted by the wind like a thin yellow flag off her belly. "The people who lived here."

"I don't know. Maybe. Indians. Snow. Fever. Smallpox. Any number of things. But there's no graveyard, is there? Which makes me think they probably just moved on."

"That's not as fun to think about."

"Don't get melodramatic on me, Tom. We'll never survive the week."

She made a visor with her hand and looked across the empty grass and around behind the house to a single section of standing rail fence.

"That's where they tie up the ghost horses at night," he told her.

"Is this what your cabin is like?"

"I've told you what it's like."

"Will we have horses?"

"Look, Tom. I know I'm a handsome guy and all, but you're not invited to stay that long."

"I was just pretending."

"Long as we're both clear on that." He turned over his wrist and read his watch. "Five days from now we'll be driving back the other way, delivering you to your loving mother, and—"

"—none of this ever happened." She rolled her eyes. "I know."

He dropped his hand and gaped at her. "That's not what I was going to say. Never happened! Tommie. Of course it will have happened. It's happening now. Isn't it?"

"Duh."

"That's right. And eventually—maybe not right away, but eventually—you'll tell everyone about it. Right?"

She snorted. "Yeah, right. I'd be dead meat."

"So you wait till you're eighteen. Or twenty-six. Right now you're just eleven."

"Don't remind me."

He lifted her chin with his hand. "Eleven is the most perfect age to be a girl. And you'll know it the minute you turn twelve."

He took her arm and they circled the falling house, stepping carefully through the high grass, lifting their knees as though walking through deep snow.

They came to the ragged edge of dry weeds and he opened the fence and she stepped through.

The truck was straight ahead, tilted on the shoulder. He nodded at it. "Race you back?"

He beat her to the highway by twenty yards and stood at the truck with his hands on his thighs, watching her come as if she hadn't already lost, her little white fists pumping high at the sides of her flat, narrow chest.

"That's a sign of a real athlete," he said when she reached him. "That's what you call running through the line."

She leaned on her knees, breathing hard. "It's hard to run."

"We're higher up. Even though it looks flat here," he said, "there's less oxygen. It makes it harder for your body to maintain itself."

"Like you can hardly run?"

"Like you can hardly run."

He ran his sleeve across his forehead and leaned on his thighs, looking at her. "When you're a mom you can tell your kids the story about passing through Cheyenne when it was a ghost town of rotted wood and wind, a fox den taken hostage by lonely teenagers, and they'll think you're ancient and wise, and you know what?"

"What."

"They'll be right."

That got him a big gap-toothed smile. He loved to see it.

"You ready?"

"Ready."

"You awake now?"

"Yep."

But in ten minutes and even with the windows down and the radio up she was asleep again, so Lamb pulled off the side of the road to wake her and stepped into the weeds to piss and back in the truck told her far to the north along the same line of longitude was a palace made of corn.

"I thought we already passed that."

"You're kind of a dreamy kid, aren't you?"

He made up a story about barrel racing in the town of Gillette when he was a boy and he told her he was a great ballplayer, second base, and a track star.

"Hurdles," he told her. "I won all the medals."

"I bet you were one of the cool kids." She had

her head leaned back against the long strap of the seat belt.

"Ever heard the term road weary?"

"No."

"Well. That's what you are. Or no. I'll tell you what it is. The gods getting back at you for being such a pig last night. Stealing both pillows and keeping me up with your snoring."

"I do not snore."

"How do you know? Ever share a room with someone before?"

"No."

"Well then."

"Last night was like a thousand years ago."

"Well we've entered mountain time. Happened in Nebraska."

"What's that?"

"I'll tell you what it is. It's mysterious."

They reached the next filling station by early afternoon, a mile north of the highway at the edge of a small town encroached upon in all directions by a shimmering flood of weeds. It was an old 76. The concrete foundation was tilted ten degrees, and once bright letters on a placard for soft-serve ice cream were drained of color. Inside he bought the girl a coffee and told her she was grown up enough for a full cup. Told her that the dire circumstances of her weak brain and laziness required it. They both laughed and she filled the cup with sugar and half a dozen little plastic cups of vanilla creamer.

Lamb went into the men's room to order a round-trip plane ticket from Chicago to Denver—for Linnie—and when he came outside he found the girl crying quietly beside a greasy trash can spotted with rust. Snot glistening on her upper lip. On the far side of the parking lot a woman was helping a tiny girl into a bright blue windbreaker. Lamb stood beside Tommie and together they watched the mother buckle the child into the backseat of a white minivan. In a moment they were gone, a speck disappearing up the frontage road and turning onto the eastbound highway.

He put his arm around her shoulders and when she turned to look up at him he stooped beside the trash can and took her face in his hands and brushed the tears from her freckled cheeks with the edge of his sleeve, wiped the snot from her lip with his thumb and wiped it on his jeans. "Do you want to go home, Tommie? Shall I take you home to your mother?"

"Yes." Her chest broke open now and she snorted and inhaled stuttering breath. "No." She looked to him for help.

"Come," he said. "Come get in the truck. Let's talk." He took her hand and walked her there. In the Ford he put the cell phone in the glove compartment and closed it. "We'll turn around. We'll drive straight through the night, okay? You can walk home from that pretty white hotel where we stayed, or I'll give you taxi money. You can go back to the apartment and all your friends. Tell your mom you wandered off into the woods and fell asleep for days. Like a pretty little girl in a fable."

She sat nodding and sniffling in the passenger seat.

"I'm sorry, Tom. This was a bad idea. I should have known better. People don't do this, do they? This isn't the way people behave. I'm older and I should have known better."

The girl held her head in her hands. "I'll get in so much trouble."

"No you won't. You won't. Everyone will be so happy to see you. You need to just let me steer this now. I'm going to feed you really well and we'll set you up in back so you can sleep and before you know it you'll be waking up in your old neighborhood."

"Okay."

"And I'll leave town so you have all the room you need to get over this. Nine hundred days and the whole city to yourself. Maybe I'll drive back through Chicago in a few years, and you can sneak away from your boyfriends and girlfriends to give your poor old horse a little company. Come steal him away from his tall metal hotel downtown, right? Have a run through the open grass before we sneak you back in time for algebra. Right?"

"I want to stay. I want to stay." She waved her hand at the windshield. "Go," she said. "Drive."

Our guy picked up her hand. "We're just going to sit here a minute." He waited until she stopped crying, then pulled away from the gas pump and parked beside a derelict pay phone. "We are not going to do anything unless I am absolutely certain it's what you want to do." She nodded and wiped her nose across her skinny bare forearm. "Oh no," he said, "don't do that." He opened the glove compartment and withdrew a handkerchief. "Here," he said. He dabbed her tears and held it to her nose. "Blow," he said. "Go on." She looked at him, red-eyed and ugly. "Harder," he said. "Yes. Now that's a nose-blow. That's a girl with a little strength!" He dropped his hand into her lap. "My God," he said, looking at her, "that's the most extraordinary sound I've ever heard. You sound exactly like a goose, or a loon. Do it again." He lifted the handkerchief, and they both laughed.

"Better?"

"Better."

He rolled down both windows and turned off the engine. The sound of passing cars and birdsong filled the truck. "All right," he said. "Let's try to talk about this rationally. What are the facts?"

"I'm being a baby."

"That's not a fact. That's an interpretation, and not one with which I particularly agree. Let me give you an example of a fact. We're in north South Dakota. Fact."

"Okay. It's early evening."

"Hey." He raised an eyebrow. "That was a pretty little sentence, Tom."

She smiled.

"What else have you got?"

She paused and looked him in the eye. "I'm running away from home."

Lamb widened his eyes. "You are?"

She looked down at the handkerchief, twisted in her hands. "Maybe."

"Oh, Tommie." He stared out the windshield. "I don't know how that makes me feel."

Nothing.

"You could have told me that was what you were doing. Did you think I wouldn't let you come with me?"

"Yes."

"Tell me the truth."

"I thought you wouldn't let me because I don't want to go back."

"But right now you do want to go back."

"I feel bad!" Her voice rose to a thin, hysterical pitch and she was crying again.

"Ssh. I know. It's okay. Listen. Listen, Tom. Do you remember our deal?"

"We spend a week, then you take me back."

"Almost."

"We spend a few days and you take me back."

"That's correct. And is that running away from home?"

She shook her head.

"That's like a vacation, right?"

"But a secret vacation."

"Well. I don't know how I feel about the word secret. It's more like the kind of thing a teenager would do, right? A teenager vacation."

She wiped her nose with the handkerchief.

"And you agreed to this deal."

"Yes."

"No running away."

"No."

"Good," he said. "I don't know how it makes me feel, that you were keeping this from me."

"I'm sorry!"

"Hey now, hey now." He ran his hand from her forehead into her hair. "Take it easy. I was a teenager too, once. Ten thousand years ago. I know what it's like. And I bet seeing that mom and her little girl gave you a little bruise right here, right?" He pressed her breast with his thumb, right where her heart would be.

She nodded.

"Well, let's talk about this. Because if you feel bruised about something you didn't even do—like run away—then our trip is off to a pretty shaky start. And we have to get it back on track together. Okay?"

"Okay."

"Tom, look at me. Good girl. Can you give me a smile? I love to see that. Good. Now tell me if you feel like you're running away."

She shook her head.

"Why not?"

"Because I'm going back in a few days."

"You're not abandoning your mother."

She shook her head, lips pulled into her mouth and her eyes filling up again, and he put his hands around her face and drew in close, his breath warm and steady on her mouth and nose and chin.

"No. You're not. She is probably worried, but we'll send a postcard, and she'll get it tomorrow, or maybe the next day, and that will make her feel a lot better." He held her face close and spoke nearly into her mouth. "And by the time she gets worried again, you'll be knocking at the door. A little more mature, a little wiser. Your beautiful long hair kissed with October sun from being so high up in the mountains. And she'll be able to see all this, won't she?"

"Yes."

"And it will be such a relief to her, that you're growing up wise and straight and tall." His voice a soft and easy rush against her face.

"Yes."

"And she'll love you more than ever. And you'll love her more than ever."

"Yes."

"There is room enough in your heart, Tom, for more love than you know, okay?" He looked directly into her eyes. She glanced up, and down again to the thin yellow stripe across the chest of his shirt, and back up again.

"Okay."

"That probably doesn't mean much to you now, but I want you to remember that I said it. I want you to remember that your heart includes everything. It is very, very big. No matter what gets in there— bad feelings, sorry feelings, ashamed feelings—you don't have to cast it out. You just let your heart contain it all."

"Okay."

"I sound a little funny, don't I?" He backed up, releasing his hands from her face. She smiled and nodded. "How are we doing now? Should we go back to our facts?"

She nodded.

"I'll start. Here's a fact: you blow your nose like a honking loon."

She laughed. "You make me laugh."

"Oh, sweetheart. That's my favorite fact of the day." He smiled broadly and took her face in his hands again and kissed her forehead. "Is that okay? If I do that?"

"Yeah."

"Okay," he said, sitting up straight. "I think that made me blush a little. Did that make you blush?"

"A little."

He smiled. "How about this one: we're almost there."

"We are?"

"Another fact: this is the only time you and I will ever be in his truck together, in the middle of the day, at the skirt of the mountains."

"We could go west or east."

"Eventually, come hell or high water, Tom, you're going back east."

"I think we should go on to the Old El Rancho Road."

He raised a hand. "Now don't be so hasty, Tommie. If you change your moods so fast, I'll feel like you don't really know what you want. Like you're too young for this. I'll get to thinking you're just saying what I want to hear."

"Oh."

"Listen, dear. It is of the utmost importance to our friendship—to me—that I not feel like a bully here. Okay?"

"But I really do think we should go."

"Let's do this. Let's park this truck across the street—see that place over there?" It was an empty boarded-up restaurant made of dark slabs of wood and fashioned with a porch to resemble a general store. "Then we'll take a walk. Just to clear the air a little, right? And when we get back to the truck, we'll make a decision."

Outside the air was cool and bright yellow. Lawns around the houses were deep and soft, the air fragrant with sweet and rotting cow manure. A metal sprinkler ticked and a few kids in dirty T-shirts were circling each other on their bikes in the middle of the wide street. Crickets and frogs in the muck-filled retention ponds were in full chorus, the faces of the tiny houses blinking blue and gold-lit windows.

"Pretty little town."

"Yeah."

"I wish I could buy your mother a house like that. In a town like this. Or like one of those, with a glassed-in porch. With a bedroom from where you can hear the train whistle in your sleep. And a little breakfast nook downstairs for hot rolls and coffee in the morning."

"That'd be the day."

"Tell me," he said and held up his face to her. "Is it a good face?"

The girl shrugged. "Sometimes I think maybe this is just a movie we're in."

"No, Tommie, this is real. Real arms. Real legs. Real trees."

"Okay."

"None of this will matter to you the way it should if you start thinking it's just some movie. You're not pretending, are you?"

"No."

"Promise?"

She laughed. "Swear."

"What I was going to ask you," he said, "was if your mother would like my face. Because wouldn't that be the perfect solution," he said, "to our little problem?"

The girl tipped her head at him. "I don't know what you mean."

"Maybe when we get back, when I take you back, we could rig things so I meet your mother. What do you say to that?"

"Yeah."

"Maybe—and I don't want to get ahead of myself here, because you'd have to say yes first—but maybe we could have a small, private wedding. On a green green lawn. Or no. In a house with big windows, and all snowy outside. And beautiful fine china, and roasted duck. Right? And your mother in a beautiful white cape. And you in red velvet. Or blue. What do you think? Blue or red?"

"Red."

"And I'll buy her a big beautiful house and get her three maids just to help her dress in the morning, and she'll never have to work another day in her life. How about that?"

"Oh, my God, she'd love you."

"And we'll have horses."

"But maybe you wouldn't like her face."

"I think I've already seen it."

"You have?"

"Does she have short dark hair?" He made a motion with his hands, cutting the hair at chin length.

"Yes."

"I have to make a confession, Tommie. Don't be mad. I went over there the night you were waiting for me at the hotel."

"To ask if I could go with you?"

"What? No. No, not like that. I just wanted to think about whether it was a bad idea, what we were about to do. I wanted to put my face right up to the facts: that you're eleven, and your parents—your mom—would be waiting for you in the apartment. I wanted to make myself really think about that. You understand?" He turned to face her.

"Yes."

"It's the only way to do this. We have to be honest about these things."

"I know."

"I saw a young woman and man there. I thought maybe it was your mom and Jessie."

"Probably it was."

"And Tom, here's my real confession, okay?" She watched him. "Ever since that moment?" He paused and looked up.

"What?"

He looked at her. "Ever since that moment, Tom, I've been haunted by her beauty."

"My mom?"

"Your mother, yes. Don't you think she's beautiful?"

"I guess."

"You guess. Let me tell you something. She is. And I'm an expert on such matters."

"I know."

"You do?"

"You already told me that one."

He put his thumb and forefinger beneath her chin and lifted her face. "Look at me. We know the facts, right?" She nodded. "And we're proceeding with due caution, right?"

"Yes."

"Because we love this world. And everybody in it."

"Yes."

"Good." He let go her head, put his hand on top of her hair. "So we're all saddled up pushing on. Because it's what people like you and me do."

. . . . .

He drove into the night, along a cursive pass etched in granite, above the stands of green-fingered oaks and red-beaded hawthorns and all the aspen, above the trees that listed to the southeast, needled black along one side, twisted and deformed by forbidding glacial wind, and between great planed walls of rock dressed in little aprons of snow and shattered stone sliding down onto the road.

The rock walls flattened as they crested the pass, and they slowly descended through the sparse coniferous trees, silver needles flashing mutely in the

car light. They wound down past the neon yellow
road signs and steep grade warnings and through
the pines again and back to where the aspen were
still yellow and pale green.

"It's scary up here."

"Well." He watched the road. "It's severe, is what
it is. And high."

"How high?"

"Twelve, thirteen thousand feet. That's over two
miles high."

"I know that."

"I forget sometimes how smart you are." He
glanced at her and back to the road. "Know what
happens now that we're over the top of the mountain? All the rivers start running the other way."

"Big whoop."

"And birds over here are much bigger. Turkey
vultures and eagles and owls and hawks."

"Bears?"

"Yes. And cattle."

"We've seen that."

"Not like this. Over here, they're twice the size,
and all over the mountains, in the trees, and swimming in the creeks up to their necks."

"No way."

"Forest cattle."

"You're lying."

"In late fall, guys like me come out and hunt hamburger."

"Yeah, right."

"You watch," he said. "See if you don't catch a glimpse of huge furry cows peering back at you through the trees, their beautiful velvet ears stapled with plastic tags, thick straight hair hanging down around their faces."

"I love this."

"Oh, you dear." He glanced at her again. "That is the best thing I've heard in years." For a minute he was quiet. "It really is," he said. "And don't think that's an easy thing to admit."

He let her drift in and out of sleep until they came to a tiny town perched on the green slopes of a little river valley. It was very cold, clear black. Huge wind scraped through the dark grassy bowl, rocking the truck where he parked it outside a small, dim-lit motel. Tommie snoozed in the warm truck while he checked them in, and when he opened the passenger door for her and she stepped out, the wind took her off balance.

"Calling Mr. Sandman," he said, catching her beneath the arm.

"Don't," she said, looking up at him, the whites of her eyes bright in the dark. "I hate that guy."

"I know," he said. "Me too."

"Where are we?"

"Encampment."

"It's so dark."

"Look up."

"Whoa." They stood in the open, she leaning against him, tucked into the crook of his arm, a wash of stars spilling above them. "I've never seen so many."

"I know you haven't." Their chins tipped up in the dark.

"It makes you feel like, what way is up?"

"It doesn't get like this at home. Not with all those city lights." He squeezed her closer. "Come on. Let's get out of the cold."

He took their gear and led her through a flimsy, blue-painted motel door and locked it behind them. It was musty, reeked of cigarettes and Pine-Sol. Lamb cranked up the heat and went into the bathroom counting backwards while she took off her blue jeans and yellow sweater and folded them carefully over the back of the chair and climbed into one of the double beds. The toilet flushed, the bathroom door opened.

"Asleep already?"

"Mmm."

"I had an idea." He picked up her unfinished coffee and carried it over to the bedside. She shook her head, eyes closed. "I thought we could write postcards."

She opened her eyes. "To my mom and Jessie?"

"And Jenny and Sid."

She wiggled up against the pillow. "Can't we do it in the morning?"

He bent over her to fluff the pillow and held the Styrofoam cup to her lips. "Come on," he said. "One good gulp will fuel you and I won't be lonely till I get tired, right?"

She turned her head and caught the cup with her hand, pushing it away, dumping half the cold muddy coffee down her chest. Coffee beaded on the bedspread and ran down her chest and bare arm.

"Oh." His voice came out in a whisper. "It's all over you."

She held the blanket with both hands and shut her eyes. Outside the wind knocked over a metal trash can, its hollow metal rolling across the far side of the parking lot.

"Okay," he said. "Don't move. You'll get coffee on your blankets and I'm not sharing mine with you." He took the edge of the blanket and she let it go. He pulled it back and looked away. "Come on," he said. "Up and into the bathroom." She reached for the blanket. "Tommie, you can't sleep like that. Now come on, I'm not looking." He reached down to the nightstand and turned out the light. He scooped her up and she jerked, catching him in the cheekbone with her elbow. Just a loose elbow. An accident.

"Goddamn it, Tommie." He took her wrist. "Christ, that hurts."

"I'm sorry!" Her strange little face twisted up, her eyes small and white and wet in the dark.

"I've got you, okay? And I can't see you. So just relax." Her body was rigid and shook with noiseless crying. "Boy," he said, crossing the room, "you walloped me." He carried her into the bathroom and turned the water knob with his bare foot and ran his toe beneath the faucet. "You like it good and hot or a little cooler?" Now she was clinging to him.

"I don't want a bath. Please, I don't want one."

"Don't be embarrassed." Something about the dark made him whisper. "You're covered with coffee. Look. It's all dark. I can't even see you."

"You. Can. Feel me." Her chest heaving in his arms.

"Oh, come on, Tom." The bath filled with water.

"Why. Don't you. Go outside and count?"

"Why don't I what? Oh, Tom, I'm stupid. That's exactly what I should have done. I'm going to put you down right now and do that, okay? It's just me. Just your friend Gary."

She nodded.

"Good. Okay, now careful. Don't punch me again!" He pushed the hair back off her wet face and he lowered her down. "Is this okay? Tell me it's okay. We'll take a quick bath and you'll sleep better. You can sleep all day tomorrow if you want. Right? Is it okay?" He lowered her down. "Do you want to do it yourself? Can you do it yourself? Is it safe to leave you here all upset?" He tried to hold her as she leaned over to step into the tub, but she twisted away from him and fell in, smacked her head against the porcelain edge. He went down on his knees. "Oh, Christ," he said, fumbling in the bathtub for the rubber stopper. Now her chest and throat broke open with crying and he was worried about people in neighboring rooms. "Ssh," he said. "Ssh. What happened? What is this? Did you bite your tongue?" Blood on her chin. The tub filling with water. "Tommie, please," he said. "I'm sorry. Christ, tell me you forgive me. Oh God, you can't trust me. Do you see how you can't trust me?" He was whispering, the faucet roaring, and the girl crying and shaking in the tub, her hand over her mouth.

"You have to get out of those clothes. If I leave you in here, you put those clothes on the edge of the tub and I'll hang them to dry, right?" Her underwear. "Tom. Tom, I can't understand you, take a deep breath." He put a hand on her back and breathed out, sighing. "Ahhh," he said. "Right? Deep breath. Ahhhh. Can I leave you here?"

Nothing. Shuddering breath.

"Listen, Tommie. I'm going to help you, okay? Real quick. We'll just soap you up and go to sleep, right?" He tore open the paper on the soap bar and set it on the edge of the tub. "Here," he said. "Lift up your bottom." She did not move. "Okay, Tom. You're a big girl. You can do this yourself. I'm going to walk out of this bathroom, lights out, and you take off that tank top and your underwear and leave them on the edge of the tub right?"

"I want." She sniffed. She ran her hand beneath her nose and her arm came away streaked with snot and blood. "To go home."

"No," he said. "No you don't. Here." He held up her hands and lifted off her tank and held his breath. "I'm not looking," he said. "I give you my word. I'm just giving you a bath, right?" She nodded. "Now slide those off. There you go. Good girl. Oops. Oops. Get the other leg. Good. Okay. Now soap," he said. "Soap soap." He put it in her hand. "Ssh," he said. "Ssh. Lather that up. You know how to do it. This is fine, right? Just like a father would do if you were sick, right? Or if you bumped your head. Let me see your chin. Is it bad? Stick out your tongue." She sat there holding the soap, so he took it back and rubbed his palms with it, his hands shaking. And he washed her. Scooped up warm water to splash over her shoulders. He cleaned her face. He talked the whole time, not stopping, and she hung forward and he soaped her back and lifted one arm at a time and underneath the arm and across the chest, mechanically, coldly, like a nurse. "That's it," he said, singing, "nice and clean. Then we'll sleep in and sleep all day tomorrow. We can just stay here all day and sleep and watch TV and eat snacks." He turned off the faucet. The room went dead quiet. Small splashing of bathwater. He picked up her feet and soaped her toes and ankles and calves and ran the bar of soap up beneath her thighs and around her bottom moving fast, every inch of her body as smooth as the inside of her arm. "We'll pull down the blinds and double up the pillows and blankets and just sleep." Whispering now. Small splashing of bathwater. "You can curl up right against me. You can snore away and"—he filled his hands with warm water and spilled it over her head—"dream and dream." He stood and took a cellophane-wrapped cup from the bathroom sink. "Let me wash your hair and I'll tuck you in. Just like you were my girl. Just like you were my very own. Now. Here you go. Yes just stretch right out. Lean—yes. Put your head in my hand. There you go. Relax. Yes." And he was filling her hair with warm sloshes of water and with shampoo and he rubbed her scalp in small soapy circles, and the water lapped in the dark and he felt her let the weight of her head go into his hand. "Do you want to be my daughter for the week?" He was saying. "My very own?"

She nodded her wet, soapy head in his hands, and it was fine, she was fine, he rinsed her hair, filling the plastic motel cup with warm water and pouring it over the top of her head. "Yes," he was saying, "let me wash you, sweetheart, let me put you to sleep."

. . . . .

When the girl woke the road was running beneath her. Sky painfully brilliant through the windshield. "I thought I was dreaming," she said suddenly and sat straight up. She was in the yellow sweater and her old sneakers and dirty blue jeans. Outside the truck, before and beside and behind her, an endless span of blond grass and silver bitterbrush and greasewood and sage. All of it vast and unchanging, as though Lamb and the girl were at rest and not rushing west, a diffuse and unmappable destination toward which they sped on an otherwise empty state highway.

"You *were* dreaming." Lamb looked over at her, his cheekbone a soft shining purple, blue eyes bright. He was in a clean shirt, face scrubbed, hot coffee and a boiled egg in his belly, and the open road before him. "Boy, did you ever sleep, my pretty little pig. Were they good dreams?"

She looked out the window, then back to him, to the bruise on his face. "No." She crossed her arms over her chest and looked back outside. "Where are we?"

"North Dakota."

"I want to go home."

"No you don't. Don't be that way. Here." He reached into the glove compartment and pulled out a giant chocolate chip cookie wrapped in Saran Wrap. "You hungry?" She turned her head, and he put it on her lap. "You have a good internal clock," he told her. "Anybody ever told you that?"

Nothing.

"Well," he said, "put it on the list of amazing characteristics of the amazing girl you are." She kept silent. "Don't you want to know why I think you have a good internal clock?"

Shrug.

"Because you slept two full days and woke up just in time to see the street sign." The mouth of a narrow dirt road broke through the shrub without warning, an opening in the brush and scrappy trees that anyone but our guy would have missed. He slowed the truck almost to a stop and turned and pointed: El Rancho Road.

"Two days?"

"I wanted to show you the Royal Gorge. But you wouldn't wake up."

"Two days?"

"Then I wanted to show you Rabbit Ears Pass. But you told me go to hell and take my rabbit with me. Did you know you talk in your sleep?"

She started to cry. She pulled the handle of the door again and again. "You said two days on the road."

"I miscalculated."

"I want to go home."

He stopped the truck and put it in Park.

"I did not sleep two days. Unlock the door. Why do you put the child lock on? I'm not a little kid." Her voice high and fast and tight again. "Open it."

"Where are you going to go?"

"I don't know. I don't care."

"You fell asleep at the top of that mountain. Do you remember? It was all dark and you said it was scary and I told you to shut your eyes. Just sleep. Do you remember?"

"You're never going to take me back."

"Tommie. Tommie Tom Tommie. We can go back right now. Is that what you want to do?"

"I don't believe you." She put her face in her hands and talked into them. "I did not sleep for two days." She looked again at the bruise.

"Well. I don't know what to say about that. I think you were pretty tired that night at the motel."

"You think I'm stupid and you treat me like I'm five." She crossed her arms over her chest, tears still coming. "I don't need fucking baths."

"Hey." He raised his voice. "Watch your language. I know how old you are."

"Well, why don't you act like it?'

Lamb took the car out of Park.

"So you're just going to keep driving anyway?"

"There's no way to turn around on this narrow road without going to the end where it widens. I'll take you back. You want to go back? I'll send you. And so much for all this." He flung his hands up. "So much for all this." They wound through a stand of cottonwoods and round bushes with waxy yellow flowers all hunched together over an empty arroyo. The road was pitted and narrow and wash-boarded, dipping and rising again. Long-stemmed spikes of yucca already dried out by cold nights and wind rattled in the breezes. The girl turned away from Lamb and leaned her forehead against the cool glass. She shut her eyes. For five minutes they rolled slowly over the uneven road.

"Talk to me, Tommie. What is it? You're all finished now? You want to go home really?"

"Like you would really let me."

"I promised you a plane ticket if you want one and we can go straight from here to the little airport and put you on a propeller plane and good night, Tommie. Is that really what you want to do? Just say. I'll give you a little purse of money and a bag of snacks and cash for a cab from Midway to Lombard." The left front wheel dropped five or six inches into a gouge of dirt and they jerked in their seats. He gave her a look. Contrite. "I'm sorry, Tom. I am. I'm not very good at this. I've never had a niece, or a sister, or anything like that. To say nothing of a daughter. This is new territory for me, do you understand? That's part of the beauty of this thing, isn't it?"

Nothing.

"Can't you find it in your heart to forgive me?"

She said nothing.

"You can say no, if you want to. That's how it's going to be—where we say everything we're thinking. Especially things that are hard to say. Promise you'll always tell me those things. And the stupid stuff. Everything. I want to know when you're homesick. When you're cold. Or like, when you have diarrhea."

"Ew." She made a face.

"Come on," he said. "You've had diarrhea, haven't you?"

Her mouth was twisted into a crinkled bud. Trying not to laugh.

"Don't pretend you haven't. Where it tears up your belly and it feels like someone is slicing your guts with a lawn mower blade, and it's all messy and it burns your butt and it's terrible, right?"

"Oh, sick." But she was smiling now.

"I want to know when you have it next. And I want to know when you need to vomit, so I can hold your hair back and brush your teeth for you, right? We don't have to be big and bad and tough with each other, do we? It's not like that, is it? Aren't we friends? Don't friends make mistakes and miscalculations and still they're friends?"

"I guess."

"You're embarrassed because I saw you naked. No. I know you are. And I'm sorry. I'd take off all my clothes now too, but I don't think you want to see it."

She looked out the window away from him, smiling at the glass.

"Look at this. Would you look at this? Is this the most beautiful place on the planet or what? Look—look—another hawk. Do you see that wingspan?" He tipped his head beside the steering wheel and watched it spiraling up into the blue sky.

"Did I bruise your eye?"

"Why? You want to even them out?"

"Maybe."

"You think about it. And let me know what you decide."

"Gary."

"Tom."

"You don't have to turn around."

"Listen. Don't make your mind up yet. Jury's still out on the truck driver, right?"

She watched him. He put the truck in Park and opened his arms. "Will you give me a hug?" She let him enclose her. "Are we making up?" She nodded her head in his shirt. He pushed her away and looked at her. "Favorite girl," he said and pulled her back in. "Favorite girl favorite girl."

. . . . .

"Are you ready? Because this is going to change your life."

"I'm ready."

"Get up on your knees in the seat."

"On my knees?"

"Right. Like that. Keep your eyes closed."

"Like this?"

"Perfect. Give me a second."

"What are you doing?"

"Turning off the engine."

"What?"

"Okay. Open your eyes."

The truck was parked in front of a sheet-metal outbuilding Lamb would call the shop. He looked at the girl. He loved to make her eyes big. Her mouth was open. Sweet. He gently pressed a finger beneath her chin and shut it. She grinned, up on her knees, and looked all around, three hundred and sixty degrees. In the new quiet, engine off, they could hear the rush of a river. A magpie sat on the rusted weather vane and blinked. No other houses in sight. Grass and a blue sawtooth horizon and trees and somewhere out behind those trees, nothing and nothing and nothing and nothing. Lamb opened the glove compartment and took out a small ring of keys.

"Just like you imagined?"

"But"—she was whispering—"I thought we were pretending."

"We were." He got out of the Ford and pointed at the house. He pointed to the water tank off beside the shop. It was all just as he'd said. "Come on," he said. "I want to show you something."

She followed him through a brown metal door into a huge shop. He pointed to the woodstove, at the pickle jar on the workbench. She took it all in, looked at him with a huge open-mouthed smile on her little face.

"I know," he said. He crossed the room and opened the box beside the pickle jar and took out a soft pack of Marlboros and shook one out. He put it in his mouth, held it with his teeth, and led the girl across the shop to a green-painted door. "Go on," he said, "open it."

She turned the handle and there it was: the bunk beds, the old, soft sleeping bags, the nightstand.

"I think there might be something up there," he said, lifting his chin toward the top bunk. He took a matchbook out of his back pocket and lit the cigarette. She went into the small room and climbed up the bunk. On the pillow there was a brown paper package.

"What does it say?"

She kneeled on the mattress, staring. "It says my name."

"Open it."

"But Gary."

"The fewer questions you ask, the more fun this is going to be. Open it."

She lifted the package. It was a bag folded under, and out slid a blue-and-white striped nightgown. The stripes were strings of blue roses.

She made a crooked smile and climbed down with it.

"Isn't that pretty," he said.

"I've never had one like this."

"I didn't think you had."

She stood there holding it, then let it unfold and pressed it to her shoulders. "I think it's a little big."

"You'll grow into it."

She fingered the blue satin ribbon woven around the collar.

"I thought we'd go see the river."

"Can I wear this?"

He stared at her. "If you want to," he said. "It's your week."

She crossed the tiny room with the nightgown on her arm and put her hand on the door. "Go," she said. "I'll change."

She stepped out of the shop in the blue-and-white flannel nightgown lifting the hem: bare feet.

"Come on," he said. "Race you to the river."

The unpaved county road curved northwest in a pale dirt hook, so when Lamb led the girl across toward the river, he could see the white of another house ahead. Just under a mile up the road.

"Gary," Tommie whispered and stopped. She pointed to the other side of the river, beyond which lay a field of yellow-green and gray grass into which several does and a four-point buck dipped their heads. Lamb nodded as if he knew they'd be there, as if he'd planned the whole thing, the deer, the bend of flyaway grass, the red-branched willow striping the blue sky. He smiled down at her as if to say: didn't I tell you so? They walked on, stepping over saltbush, their footsteps crackling through the dry grass, scaring up field mice and finally alerting the mule deer, which went tearing off toward the low distant line of foothills.

Our girl stood and looked into the water, the tapering branches of water birch quaking behind her. "Can we swim?" Her belly stuck out a little beneath the clean and bright white flannel, freckles multiplying by the trillion on her cheeks and on the backs of her hands, and he wanted to reach out and freeze her, stop her just as she was. Seize her from the woman who would steal her away a day at a time. The river water was as low and as clear as it would be all year but still broke white over small piles of rocks. Yellow grass blew slowly in the bright shallows. He could see her cracking her head, could imagine too poignantly the turn in the story that would leave him with a dead girl on his hands.

"It's not deep enough. Look at those rocks."

"Oh."

"We can fish, though."

"Oh."

"That doesn't interest you?"

"I don't like fish."

"Well, you've never had it right out of the river. When you eat it like that, it turns all your skin just the faintest silver."

"You're weird."

"No, I'm serious."

"Will it cover up my freckles then?"

"It will brighten them into blinding points of light."

"Can I be like Medusa where it kills people?"

"You don't get to make up the laws of the universe."

"I thought that was the game."

"Oh, my dear." He stooped and reached into the cold water and pulled out a smooth stone. "This is not a game." He held it out for her to kiss and skipped it down the river.

"Forget it, then." She stooped to find a stone. "I don't want any fish."

Small drab birds hid in the red willow and tore upward in a flash of blue light. The embarrassing drip and splash of river water. Birds splitting open the quiet with clear and high-pitched calls. The hollow rush of wind. The ruffled hem of her nightgown lifting in the breeze, catching on the grass.

"Do you want to put your feet in the river?" he asked.

Alison Foster saw them standing like that, the knee-high grasses waving and billowing like yards of silk at the backs of their knees. He watched the man run his hand through the girl's hair and tousle it on top. He watched her run from him, and he heard her high small laugh and the low hum of his response. Sunlight glanced off the child's hair in a bright ring on the crown of her pale head. Foster cleared his throat. Lifted his trembling face at them. "This is private property," he said.

The girl started, but Lamb, shielding his eyes with his hand, turned toward the skinny old man. "That's my property." He grinned.

Just as Lamb was about to put a hand on the child's head, she slipped her hand into his. His heart rose in his chest and up into his neck. "My niece Emily," he told Foster, who offered no comment on either the girl's nightgown or the bruise on Lamb's face. He looked down at her, indicating her bare feet. "That ain't safe." The girl said nothing. He turned to Lamb. "You here for a while? The place needs some maintenance."

Lamb smiled. "We're just here the week. At least, that was the plan. Em was just saying she'd like to stay forever."

"Not much of a place for a girl."

"I like it," Tommie said.

"Well." He gave her a thin smile. "Girl doesn't get to choose where she lands, do she?" He looked at Lamb. "How old?"

"Almost twelve," she answered.

Foster ignored her. Lamb looked at her and back to the old man. "She's eleven." Foster nodded. "Em, why don't you give us a minute? Go on and give those city feet another good rinsing." The girl nodded and went back to the edge of the river. "Don't fall in," he called after her, then lowered his voice. "She just lost her mother," he said. "We're just here for a while to. You know. Figure out what's next."

"I'm sorry. Your sister?"

"In-law. Thank you."

"Cancer?"

"Drunk driver."

"Well, I'm sorry. That's a shame."

"She's having a tough go of it. Even here."

"Like I said. No place for a girl." They stood looking out at the river. "Terrible thing, a house in that kind of disrepair."

"Well, I'll need to come out sometime more than a week to get it all straight."

"You're taking her back east?"

"That's our plan." Lamb lifted his gaze from the river, to the nets of birch overhead. "How is Mrs. Foster?"

"We have a nurse coming twice a week from Casper."

"Oh, good. Glad to hear it."

The old man put his hands in the pockets of his Wranglers. "You-all need anything."

"Thanks."

"The place really needs cleaned. Inside and out."

"I know."

"Calhoun used to polish every beam."

Lamb smiled. "So you say."

"Gutter's coming down in the back."

"I know it. Thanks."

They shook hands, and as Foster walked back through the grass and brush, the girl looked up at Lamb from the edge of the river where she sat with her nightgown tucked up between her thighs.

"He's a jerk."

"Watch your language."

"Well, he is."

"I'm sort of the new guy in this area. Best not to ruffle his feathers. You been in a place as long as he has, you start to feel entitled."

"Entitled."

"Like everything is yours. Your river, your grass, your business."

"Since when are we staying forever?"

Lamb sat down beside her, his feet in the grass and his arms stretched out behind him. "We're not. Four days to go. Then we turn around and deliver you back to your mother. All red cheeked and your

hair full of wind and nineteen thousand new freckles on your neck and face."

"What if I want to stay longer?"

"Too bad."

"No fair."

"A minute ago you wanted to go home right
away."

"I changed my mind."

"Boy." He whistled. "You're keeping me on my
toes."

"Do I have to be Emily?"

"Don't you want to be Emily?" The flowers on
the hem of her nightgown were dark blue, wet with
river water.

"What is she like?"

"Well for one, she's extraordinarily beautiful.
The wind and the river and open space did won-
ders for her complexion." Tommie rolled her eyes.
"No, seriously. And the more she ran around outside barefoot and washed her face in the cold spigot
water and rubbed dirt into her hair, the more beautiful she became."

"What else?"

"She also became really, really smart during her
time out west. I mean wonderfully bright. Want to
know why?"

"Why?"

"She had such brilliant company."

Slow to get the joke, she smiled. "I'm hungry."

"I know. I've been sitting here wondering how I'm going to feed you. Shall we explore the grounds?"

. . . . .

It was the most natural thing in the world. Days growing shorter, autumn on its way. Pretty soon breakfasts by the fire, rinsing out the mess kit in the river water. There'd be hot chocolate in the evenings. Hauling dead wood in off the riverbank and splitting it for the woodstove. He wishing they could fix her a whole Thanksgiving dinner by campfire.

"You could do that?"

"Of course I could do that."

"With a turkey?"

"A sharp-tailed grouse. And trout from the river. And chokecherry wine."

"Wine for us both?"

"Just a taste for you."

And we should probably pause here to imagine too how things were going in Illinois. How Tommie's mother would first think Tommie was at the mall or at a neighbor's house. How then Tommie's mother would realize she had not taken a breath for days. And she would start smoking, right away, to make every breath until she died a chore and a countdown until she could be with Tom again.

And how they would interview Jenny and Sid. Investigators, social workers, their parents all in a green-carpeted room with dry-erase boards, a coffeepot, chairs arranged in a circle. How one at a time the girls are questioned, how they cry after the same question. Was it a dare? How they're apologetic and how when they're flanked by their parents they seem like a couple of kids. How a social worker would ask if they understand how much danger their friend is in. How the girls will tell them every detail they can recall: how they made fake tube tops and stapled them and dotted their arms with blue-ink freckles. How they whispered their conversations about menstruating, explaining that they were talking about things Tommie wouldn't understand. How they went bra shopping on the weekends, carried their gym clothes to and from school in Victoria's Secret bags. Telling Tommie maybe one day she'd have a reason to go in the store too. How Jenny wrote a fake love letter from Tommie to her stepdad, Jessie, and read it out loud on the bus. How they pushed her in Sid's basement closet with Luke Miller, then nicknamed her Prudie and told everyone she'd cried and covered her head with her hands and hid behind Sid's dad's raincoat. How that first day she was taken into that old guy's car it had seemed, yes, unwillingly. The color of the Ford. The height of the man. His hair color. Who he looked like on TV. That Tommie wasn't taking the bus anymore after that. That Jenny saw her trace the letter G on the floor with her shoe, over and over and over again, straight through a history class. How they would be looking for Geralds, Grants, Garys, Genes, Glens with registered navy blue Ford Explorers. How the social worker—with a long flat mane of strawberry blond hair graying at the temples—didn't believe any of it. A handsome man who looks like some TV star befriends this unremarkable girl and takes her away? A man like that isn't missed by his family? His boss? His wife, say? The whole thing told like a story made up by a child.

And let's say Jessie stepped up to the plate, really started leading the team. Really found he missed her, really expressed how fond he was of the child, how he missed her affection. That's what he would call it: affection. How when investigators talked to him they would be thinking he himself could have done it, he could have taken her and hidden her away somewhere, he could be that guy. How vividly he could imagine it all. How he could be a suspect.

How he was glad she wasn't his real daughter because how would he have felt, being a man himself and knowing what was likely happening to her? He could never have held that up.

And we could say too that it was all the kids talked about at school for three days, a week, even two weeks, but how—true to a promise David Lamb would make her—Tommie would become a ghost, and everyone would forget her. All but one boy, say, a friendless scrawny kid with a perpetually runny nose and zealous parents, and who'd had a secret crush on Tommie for years, sat next to her in math and always hid his pencils before class so he could ask her for one. Say Tommie never would have mentioned this to Jenny or Sid, but she always packed an extra for him. Say she even let him borrow Lamb's little silver pencil sharpener and square-danced with him in gym class—pretending, when Jenny and Sid called for it—to be repulsed by his skinny damp hands. His life would be touched by Tommie's disappearance, how he would come to understand that this was how the universe worked. Maybe his parents would move to Nashville or Buffalo or Dallas before he could find out what happened to Tommie in the end. He'd keep his adult life empty, steeled against perpetuating the shock and horror of finding she'd been abducted. Say that was the word they were using: abducted.

· · · · · ·

The cabin was a single large room—a tiny kitchen sink and square foot of countertop, a fold-out couch, a cot, a propane heater and a propane stove. It smelled like dust and vaguely of urine and natural gas. Mouse shit seeded the floor.

"If I come back here to stay," Lamb told the girl, who held her hand over her nose, "there'll be some cleaning."

There was a tiny bathroom: sink and toilet. The water in the toilet was rust-orange, the bowl was lined with rust rings.

"Can you flush it?" She made a face.

"Wait'll I get the water turned on."

"I could clean."

"That would take years."

She shrugged. "I don't care. Are we sleeping in the bunk beds?"

"Unless you want a cot. Or a couch."

"Bunk beds duh."

For the most part the place was empty of the inventory of daily life. Some tin plates and cups and plastic dishes in the single kitchen cabinet. A split yellow sheet of paper taped to the inside door: handwritten instructions for turning on the water. Lamb tried the light switch behind the tiny porcelain sink. "Think we need electricity? We could leave the lights off."

"The whole time?"

"Look, Tom. I'll be frank with you, right? I'm always going to be frank with you." He took her by the shoulders and stooped, so they were facing each other. "Here's the thing. I feel a little funny about the possibility of that old man peeking in the windows and seeing us, and well, getting ideas."

"Like he'll know you're not my uncle."

"Exactly."

"But you act like an uncle. Even like a dad."

"Well, my dear, that's tremendously kind of you to say, but excuse me for saying I'm not exactly sure either one of us knows what a dad ought to act like."

"Oh, yeah."

"And when all the lights in a house are on and a man is outside in the dark, he can see in. Have you ever tried that?"

"Yeah."

"So."

"We'll use candles. Like the olden days."

"Whatever you want, piggy. But we're going to have to take care of some business before nightfall."

"Like lunch."

"And dinner. And ice. And a cooler. Because this guy is thirsty for a cold beer. And of course your candles. And whatever else we need. Like warmer clothes for you." He held open the cabin door and they stepped outside. "Think you can stand another hour twenty in the car? See some of the local color?" He shut the door and tried it. Locked.

"I have to get dressed."

"Yes, you do. Hey," he called into the shop after her, "don't put your shoes and socks on yet."

When she came back out barefoot and dressed in her dirty T-shirt, Lamb swooped her up and she shrieked and twisted. "Careful," he said. "You don't want to black my other eye." She let herself go like a rag doll. "Damn, kid. You're a heavy sack. What've you been eating?"

"Goose livers."

"Ah, well. Goose livers." He carried her around to the back of the Ford and opened the hatch and set her down. "Don't move."

"I won't."

"Promise?"

She crossed her chest and kissed her forefinger. "You're sweet."

She heard him go back in the shop and clanking metal and rushing water, and when he came back it was with a towel over his shoulder and a carton of powdered soap and a full plastic bucket.

The girl pulled her legs up. "No way," she said. She scooted back into the Ford. "Too cold."

"Oh, stop it." He got on his knees. "Give me your feet."

She shook her head.

He opened and closed his hand, beckoning. "Come on," he said. "Nothing comes next till you let me." She watched him. "Come on. I got a towel. Your feet are filthy. You got to wash them before you put them in your socks. What if we can't find any kid socks in town? These'll be the only ones you have all week."

She inched forward.

"Good girl." He opened the tub of soap. "We'll say that in this story you're the princess, right? And I'm just the grizzly old guy who lives in the barn and cleans your feet."

She looked out over his head while he scrubbed her feet and ankles and calves, pushing his fingers between her toes and admiring her arches. He put his fingers to her heel and lifted her foot. "It's the perfect foot," he said. "You have the perfect foot. If I were a sculptor," he said very gravely, "I could not have a conceived of a more perfect foot, Tommie."

· · · · ·

They drove an hour out. A thousand, two, three thousand feet down to a high plateau dark with trees, edges of the highway shaggy red with Indian paintbrush. Cattle wrenching yarrow from the weeds with huge square teeth. A crow perched on the shoulder of a dead pronghorn, its carcass deflated in the gravel. They drove through three cattle gates, black cows and bulls among the trees and on the hillsides and in the rocks and knee-deep in empty irrigation ditches on both sides of the highway. The two-lane widened into a four-lane. They passed a ramshackle taxidermist's, a drive-through taco stand. Tack and Feed. Snake Creek Mercantile. Pizza Hut, Sears, Kum & Go, Napa Auto Parts, and Safeway. Cardboard-colored condominiums set up in a row like empty shoe boxes, a stage set for children, a temporary game. They passed an adult boutique in a windowless concrete building. A broken metal swing set at the base of an outcropping of red-and-green striped rock. A skinny teenage girl in red-and-white dots pushing a stroller. Empty lawn chairs outside the Roundup Motel. A life-size plastic pinto rearing up from a little island of volcanic rock and weeds.

"Where is everybody?" she asked.

"Somewhere else."

Downtown was eight blocks long: little yellow, blue, and green houses with cement-slab porches, crammed among leafless cottonwoods, dirt lawns, and cracked sidewalks. There were two gas stations, one boarded up. One tall grain elevator rusted at its metal seams, a small glassless window at the top, the gaping black mouth eating rain and snow and sleet, eating all the cries and accusations the wind carries with it, of failed enterprise and family farms. A one-story brick liquor store advertising fishing and hunting licenses; a lopsided pickup in forest-service green and rotted wood-handled ranch tools scattered around it. A mom-and-pop hardware. A country kitchen. A white-painted church.

Lamb parked across the street from the kitchen, a ratty shingled awning shading red and yellow letters painted on the windows. CHICKEN-FRIED CHICKEN $3.99 and beneath that: COLD BEER $1.00. A tier of lumpy pies turned beneath an orange light in the window, and inside a huge old man in suspenders bent over his newspaper at the counter, holding his tiny white ceramic coffee mug with a massive, giant-knuckled hand. A sign posted inside the diner said ROOMS FOR RENT, and Lamb stopped in the middle of the empty street, wide for running cattle, and looked up. "You could come back here to live when you're sixteen," he said. "You could be the waitress."

"And live up there?"

"We'd get you your horse, and a flowered apron for your waitressing dress—one with long sleeves, it keeps you covered, and buttons all the way up the front. And everybody in town would know you."

"Where would I keep the horse?"

"And everyone would love you. All the patrons would want you to marry their sons and nephews and grandsons. Smart people. And you'd know all about them. Names of their children, names of their shepherds and blue heelers. Health of their old folks. And you'd go to the town meetings in long skirts, and you'd pin your hair up, like women should. And smile at them with your perfect milk white teeth. And I'd stay out at the little house, all old and gray, and you'd feel sorry for me so you'd come on your horse with slices of peach pie and cold meat loaf, wouldn't you?"

"It wouldn't be because I felt sorry for you."

"You wouldn't, would you?"

"No."

"Come, dear." He took her arm. "I'm going to feed you really good."

They crossed the street, walking toward the image of a man and a girl in the windows before them as if finally, after all this travel, they were approaching themselves. There they were—hovering somewhere inside the restaurant, walking on air, looking out at their street bodies, beckoning like ghosts.

Lamb held open the swinging glass door. Flatware rang against ceramic plates from the fat man at the counter, a skinny man and his wife in a booth. Bobby Vinton played on the AM radio. The waitress was a teenage girl with a big belly and short dark hair and thick eye makeup. She led them to a small Formica table flecked with gold and topped with a chrome napkin holder, a bottle of ketchup, a bottle of hot sauce, and forks and steak knives rolled up tight in white paper napkins. Magpies lined up on the telephone wire across the street. The waitress put laminated menus on the table, just wiped and still wet.

"Okay," Lamb said. "I want you to pick out what you want, and order two of them. Then dessert."

"I'm not that big a pig."

"Yes, you are."

"What are you having?"

"Chicken-fried chicken."

"Me too."

"No mind of her own?"

"I've never tried it before."

"Oh, I see. Wants to try new things, does she?"

"So?"

"I'm just teasing you, dear. I think it's a fine choice. Know why?"

"Why."

"It was my choice."

By the time they left the diner it was early evening, chilly. They passed a bar with the outline of a neon cowboy on horseback swinging a rope, the red green yellow and electric blue light brightening against the failed day.

At the Safeway they bought a can of red chili beans, a can of ranch beans, a can of pinto beans. A dozen cans of Dinty Moore Beef Stew; little paper-wrapped cans of potted meat; a dozen flat paper-wrapped cans of sardines; raisins and jack cheese. Sliced bread; a jar of peanut butter; two pounds of bacon and three dozen eggs; a two-liter glass bottle of brown whiskey; apple juice and tomato juice. Matches. Soap. Powdered milk. Powdered cocoa. Instant coffee. Potato Buds. Shampoo and toothpaste.

"You use an adult toothbrush?"

"Yes."

"Good." He put two in the cart. "You floss?"

"Not so much." He threw in two wheels of waxed, mint-flavored floss. "You're going to use both of those before you leave."

"That's a lot."

"We're going to start you on some good habits."

"Are we staying for two years? Because we're buying enough."

"Oh, we are not. This is called preparation. This is called planning ahead. This is making sure you have everything you need and then some."

"Okay."

"It's for your sake."

"Okay."

"If nothing else we'll send you home with a bunch of loot, right? What else do we need? Did we get cashews? Are you over the cashews?"

"I'm over the cashews."

"Good."

They loaded up outside in the dark, and a mile down the road Lamb stopped again in front of another painted window. "One more stop."

He led Tommie, teeth-chattering and hugging herself in her yellow sweater, into the Sportsman's Paradise. It was faced with rough unfinished planks of dark wood, and just outside the door a plastic man with a plastic beard in a real red-and-black checked shirt held a plastic shotgun in one hand, a plastic fishing pole with reel line in the other.

"Are we going to buy a gun?"

He raised an eyebrow. "We're here for shoes, stupid."

"Hey."

"Well, come on." He nodded at her feet. "What are those? Did you think those were shoes? Who bought you those? Did your mother buy you those nine years ago?" He held open the door. "Put them both together and you don't even have a third of a shoe."

Small bells hitched to the glass door rang as they stepped in, and the store was warm and quiet. It smelled like rubber and pipe tobacco, was crowded with cardboard boxes of shoes and carousels of shirts and sweaters and jackets. Basketball hoops hung from the rafters, a line of fishing poles from the front doors halfway to the back. The brown-carpeted floor sloped beneath their feet. In the front, a man in glasses stood behind a glass counter filled with knives. He regarded them without expression, offering no greeting. Tommie followed Lamb, who took giant steps and walked brusquely to the back, promptly lifted a beige boot with yellow laces and blue rubber bottoms and waved it at the skinny pimple-faced kid in a brown vest with a white name tag that read: CLARE.

"That's a name," Lamb said. "You know that? You don't hear that kind of name anymore."

The boy reddened. "It's my grandfather's name."

"That's sweet. Listen, Clare. My daughter is going to need a pair of these good-looking boots in"—he looked again at her feet—"a seven."

"That's a boy's shoe."

"Well, do the conversion."

Clare held up the boot and looked at the girl, who nodded and shrugged. He set the boot on the counter and disappeared behind hunter-orange curtains.

"So am I your daughter or your niece?"

Lamb turned over the display boot and knocked its blue rubber bottom. "That's a good solid boot."

"Sure."

"You don't like them?"

"They're good. I like them. I never had a boy's boot before."

"They make boys' shoes better."

"Oh."

Clare came back with the boots and Lamb took the box.

"You don't want to try those on?"

"They'll be fine. What she needs now, Clare, is something to cover herself up. Don't you agree?"

Clare looked at the girl and she crossed her arms over her chest. "Women and girls," he said and pointed toward the front of the store.

"Boys?"

Clare blinked and pointed to the right.

Lamb led the way. "Okay, Miss Piggy. Pick out a jacket."

"Why boys?"

"They make all the boys' clothes sturdier, especially this kind of gear. Does that bother you?"

She shrugged. While she looked, Lamb selected matching zero-degree mummy bags, wool socks, boys' long underwear, and a guidebook on North American trees. He bought her fleece-lined mittens and a mess kit and a thermos and a backpack. Things a kid in Lombard wouldn't have. Things she deserved to have.

"You're going to have a lot of new stuff to bring back with you."

"I know."

"Lucky girl."

"I know."

He bought cartridges for a .16 and pretied flies in a box. At the glass counter in the front, the skinny clerk with gray hair and pockmarks was reading a magazine, the cover pressed open on the glass case. He looked at the flies, then ran his gaze up and down Lamb, resting it upon his bruised cheekbone, then to the girl, his face unchanging. Without taking his eyes off her he asked Lamb if he didn't want any knives. His teeth were gray.

"Knives," Lamb said. "Do we need any knives, Em?"

"What would we want a knife for?"

The man behind the counter looked at her. "Don't your daddy take you fishing?"

She shook her head and grinned. "Not yet."

"Hunting?"

"Nope."

He looked out the window at Lamb's truck. "When you get out of that vehicle, and get out on the river, or up in the mountains, you'll need a knife." The clerk looked at him. "Won't she?" He took a shining silver knife with a five-inch blade out of the case and handed it to the girl, handle first.

Lamb looked at her. "I don't know. I think your mother would kill me."

Tommie shrugged. "She won't care."

Lamb looked from the girl to the man behind the counter and into the glass. "You don't have a good knife do you, Em."

The clerk retrieved the first knife and picked up another. "Maybe you want a skinning knife."

"Something practical," Lamb said. "Something she can fold up and keep in the coin pocket of her jeans."

"Like for an emergency?" The clerk asked, splaying his open palms upon the glass.

"Yes," he said, "like that."

The clerk nodded at the case. "Go ahead and look."

Lamb looked the man in the eye. "Why don't you give us the most expensive one you have in there." The man slid open the glass doors and selected a tiny bone-handled pocketknife. Reaching over the counter, he nodded at the girl, who opened her palm. He set it in her hand.

"That's one twenty."

She weighed it in her hand—surprisingly heavy for its size. They both had the same thought: like the pencil sharpener. She nodded at Lamb, and the clerk pointed his eyes at the girl's pockets.

"You can fit that one in your Levi's," he said.

$\bullet$ $\bullet$ $\bullet$ $\bullet$ $\bullet$

The first morning was cold, gas blue, perfect. As the light evened out above him, David Lamb leaned against the Ford in the sheepskin jacket he'd found in the cabin and listened to sporadic trills of white-throated sparrows tipping in the wind along the fence wire. Paper birch stood in thick white rows between the river and the road, straight and bare as bleached bones, their uppermost branches feathered and brain green. A headache that began as a tightening of the temple had now spread to the back of Lamb's eye, to his neck and jaw, clenched and twisted up toward the corner of his brain as if in deference to or fear of some thought lurking there. Altitude. She'd have a headache too.

He shaved in the frigid river water and scrubbed his face and nose and eyes with it, the wind like cold breath in his hair and filling his teeth and cleaning him through.

In the shop he chose a can of chili beans and five eggs and a flat tin of brisling sardines in cottonseed oil, and set everything on a flat rock behind the cabin where he'd already decided they'd make their fires. Out of Foster's view.

He lifted a bird's nest from a low slope of the gutter and tucked it under his arm. He filled his pockets with dead leaves and dried and broken grass and gathered a fistful of brittle sticks and carried it all back to camp. From the diminished woodpile in the shop he carried out the longest, narrowest logs, set them parallel in the dirt and drew two ends together, stuffing the closed point with tinder. He lit the bird's nest on fire and set it on top.

Gently he set one egg and a handful of coffee grounds into the smallest pan filled with water, then poured just a finger of brown whiskey into his tin cup. In a short while his bones were warm and the fire was cheerful and the birds were at it and his coffee was boiling. He drank the first cup slowly as he peeled the warm boiled egg in his cold hands, eating it in small bites, sipping the coffee. He was in this moment half sorry about the girl, that he'd brought her at all.

There were antelope everywhere on the ridge to the west, beyond Foster's house, their faces long and matted with shaggy white fur. Smoke from the fire rose in blue curls and woofed up into the cold and he imagined seeing it as if from a distance, the low ceiling of it thinning in a flat line beneath a slowly rising column: a signal of his presence in the world.

He refilled his cup, black this time, and opened the chili beans and spilled them into the round metal pan. His ears and fingers were stinging with cold, his nose running, his insides radiant with warmth. Shadows of grass blades in the grass blades, rising sun knitting everything together in its warmth. For the first time in a week, maybe it'd been a year, he didn't know anymore, he felt if given the chance he could really sleep.

He set the pan on the narrowest end of the fire and stirred to keep the beans from burning. One clear breaking note of birdsong. Meadowlark. The trees were luminous now, frost dissolving off the grass and off the top of the truck and here comes his girl, his little freckled daughter-niece, new sleeping bag around her shoulders. She found Lamb behind the cabin stoking a bright orange fire that stretched and shrank in the wind. There was a little pile of a mess kit beside him and a pan balanced on the pointed end of the logs.

"Come over here if you want to see the world's most perfect fire," he said. A little crooked flag of gray hair stood up on the back of his head.

She stood beside him, her face still closed up with sleep, and stared at the fire. "How long have you been up?"

"Hours. I had to make the day. One detail at a time. Very painstaking. How does it look?"

"Besides freezing?"

"It'll warm up. What do you think of the black-and-yellow bird I put over there?"

"Nice touch."

"Nice touch, she says."

"What are you drinking."

"Black coffee. We'll mix some cocoa into yours in a minute."

"I take it black."

"Do you?"

"Yes."

"How about we mix a spoonful of cocoa in today, see if you like it. We can make it stronger tomorrow."

Shrug.

"Come have a seat."

"The sleeping bag will get dirty."

"That's what sleeping bags are for. How did you sleep?"

"I forgot where I was."

"Perfect."

He moved the pans and poured cold water from a plastic gallon jug into the smallest one.

"How did you learn to do this?" she asked him.

"Been waiting about fifty years to have a breakfast just like this one. I guess in all those days I figured out pretty well how it would go."

"But you didn't know about me all that time."

"No," he said, checking the water in the pan. "You I had not planned on. You are a complete and total surprise."

"A good surprise?"

"I'm withholding any evaluative judgments for the time being."

"So you won't miss me when you take me back?"

He looked at her, his tin cup held to his lips. "Let's just have the morning, okay? No more hard questions."

He gave her the job of making toast and told her soon she'd be preparing the whole breakfast, fire and all, which she didn't believe. He latched bread slices inside a little metal cage and showed her where to hold it over the wide end of the fire.

She turned it over. "Did we buy this thing?"

"I found it here."

"Gary." She watched the bread. "Do you think my mom called the police?"

He watched the beans. "Honestly?"

"Yeah."

"Yes, I do."

"Are you going to get in trouble?"

"No."

"How do you know?"

"Two reasons. You want to hear them?"

She nodded.

"One, I'm really smart." He cracked an egg over the hottest side of the beans and set the shells in the dirt beside his boot. She grinned and studied the bread.

"I'm serious."

"So am I! Don't you think I'm smart?" He held an egg in his palm.

"Yeah," she said. "Sure."

"Good," he said. "I know you do."

"Second," she said.

He opened another egg over the beans and gestured toward the pan, the yolks of the four eggs brightening in the red beans and sauce. "Isn't that beautiful?"

She gave him a look.

"Just look at it," he said. "Think of all the chickens and bean pickers and bean canners and tomato growers and truckers in the world all collaborating to fill your belly and make you strong. It's medicine. And we're not worthy of it if we don't acknowledge it."

"Okay, it's beautiful."

"What's beautiful about it?" he asked her.

"The yellow and red."

"And all the work."

"I guess."

"All the sun and rain, which is magic."

She scrunched up her nose.

"It is, Tom. I know I'm right about this. Want to know which part has the most magic in it?"

"Which?"

"The chili peppers."

"I don't like spicy like that."

"You have to taste it carefully. With an open mind."

"But it burns my tongue."

"That's a mistaken point of view. What you're tasting in hot sauce like this is nothing less than the heat of starlight. Did you know the sun is a star?"

"Do you think I'm retarded?"

"How's your coffee?"

"Good. But not the cocoa in it."

"Honestly?"

"Yes."

"Because typically you take your coffee black."

"Yes."

"Well, then, you're my kind of girl." He pulled the pan away a little from the flames. "Don't burn our toast."

"I'm not."

"You want to hear the second reason?"

"Yes."

"This is the most important part, okay?"

"Okay."

"It's that I have you to help me. Isn't that right? I'm trusting you to help me in this. We're fifty-fifty."

"Right."

"Didn't we shake on it?"

"Yes."

"Good. So. That's how I know. Your mother and Jessie—even though you don't like him, Em, don't do that. That's a nasty habit. I hope you never roll your eyes when someone mentions my name to you."

"Sorry."

"They love you very much. How could they not?"

"I guess."

"You don't need to worry about it too much. Because this is going to be really good for everyone. It's good for their love of each other, and it's good for their love of you. And when you get back to that little apartment, and back to those girls like Jenny and Sid, there's going to be a new light about you. The stillness of the earth in you. You'll know so much more than you did. You'll know about this country's secret heart. You'll just be drenched in it. And it'll get all over everybody."

"Oh."

"Oh? Doesn't that sound good to you? Take this plate. Hold it steady. Got it? This is going to be the best breakfast of all time. Here. One, two, three eggs for you. I know how you are. Should I give you all four eggs?"

"Maybe."

"Ha. You see? Do I know everything about you, or what?"

"I know. It's totally weird."

"Taste those beans for me. Good?"

Nod. "Hot."

"How about after breakfast we pack for a little hike out toward those hills?"

"I can wear my new boots."

"We'll break them in carefully, so we don't blister your perfect white feet. And you can wear your new jacket. Unless you're going to stay in that nightgown."

"Maybe I'll wear the nightgown the whole week."

"I'd love that."

• • • • •

The best way to honor your life is to perform every act with ceremony. Don't do sloppy work. Tie your shoes carefully. Comb your hair carefully. And right

now, he said, honoring our lives means packing carefully for the hike.

"But you're packing," she said, "like we're never
coming back."

"Well, you still talk," he said, "like you think
we're in a movie."

He kneeled to the ground whenever they came
upon something new in the grass and weeds as they
hiked out through the public lands beyond the old
and abandoned ranches and along the major river.
Tiny bloodred urns of prairie smoke, animal shit
marbled with fur, and the slender bones of sparrows
and deer mice.

"See this one?" he whispered. "See those little
green hearts on the inside? The green middle? The
way they all cluster at the top here?" He made a circle
with his index finger from the petals to the stamen.

Nod.

"If we dug it up, the roots would be scaly and
black."

"No way."

"Like the hide of the devil himself."

She curled her lip.

"It's so poisonous that a single blossom would kill
someone your size."

"Whoa."

"Put you right to sleep like a princess in a fairy tale."

"How many would it take to kill you?"

He raised an eyebrow. "I'm a big guy."

"But how many?"

"More than someone like you could gather in a single day."

"I wasn't saying anything."

"Neither was I."

"What's it called?"

"I can't remember. Death something. Or deathly something. Do you want to keep one?"

"Is it poisonous to touch?"

He plucked the cluster and they held their breath, both of them eyes wide and tracing its arc through the air as he slowly lowered it between two pages of American elms in her new North American tree book. "You be careful with this."

"Okay."

"I'm serious, Em. If anyone saw it they'd know you were out west."

"Okay."

The meadow between the house and the hem of the mountains was wider than Lamb had reckoned. By the time they had crossed halfway to the swell of hill and trees, it had been nearly two hours of steady hiking, and their pants were soaked to the knees and their boots caked with manure and mud.

"If we hadn't got you those boots, we'd have had to go back an hour ago."

"Why?"

"In tennis shoes your feet would be blistered all to hell from wet socks."

"Oh."

"This is the part where you say, Gee, Gary, where would I be without you?"

"Gee, Gary, where would I be without you?"

"Tommie. Don't ever say anything like that to a man."

The passing day was marked by ravens calling, by constant twittering of song sparrows in the trees and on the fence posts. Acres of dry grass banded by red and gold ribbons of fireweed and yellow gumweed. Sagebrush grew to the height of the girl's throat, and after once lifting her over a wall of fallen alder he backed up and hurdled it.

"I can still get up there!" he said, panting on the other side, hands on his knees, grinning up into the light at her.

"You're not that old."

"Oh, say that again, you sweet child."

"You're not. You're not that old."

By noon they were climbing the ridge, the aspen groves sporadically shading the sun from their foreheads and arms.

"What are these things everywhere?"

"Cow patties."

"Cow patties?"

"Cow shit."

"There's flowers growing out of them."

"I know it. Come here. I want to put some more sunblock on your face."

"Why are they flat?"

"Cow faucet."

"Sick."

"Come here." He squeezed a white pasty worm of sunblock into his hand. "Give me your face."

"It won't help."

"I'm beginning to see that. You're a little fragile, aren't you?" He slathered her bluish white with the stuff, her skin hot to the touch, covering her face and nose and cheeks and collarbones and neck.

"I should have bought you a hat."

"Like your dad's cap?"

"A forest ranger hat. Let's get one. Let's braid your hair and get you a forest ranger hat."

"What's a forest ranger hat?"

"It's what you need. Trust me. Hey." He kneeled. "What do you think that is?"

"Footprints."

"I know that," he said. "Of what?"

"A bear?"

"No. That's from a coyote. Maybe a fox. Come here," he said, lowering his voice. "Get down here and I'll show you."

On their knees in the weeds and dust he pointed at the paw print, its tiny dashes of claws in the dirt. "See that? That means it's from a kind of dog, rather than a kind of cat."

"Like a wolf?"

"Nah. No wolves up here. Just coyotes."

"Don't they bite?"

"They won't bother us."

"When is it a cat?"

"No claw marks." He erased the claw marks with his thumb. "Like that. Got it?" And Tom. If you're out on a hike and it's a cat, like a mountain lion, you get out of town, okay?"

"Now someone behind us will think there's a lion out here."

"Is there someone behind us?"

"If there was, they'd be scared."

"Aren't we smart to make our trail safe like that?"

"Pretty smart."

"Do you think it would work in Lombard, if you drew cat prints on the sidewalk with a piece of chalk?"

She rolled her eyes.

"Maybe we could empty out the city that way," he said, standing and wiping off his knees. "We could have the whole place to ourselves."

"If there were a real mountain lion in the city," the girl said, standing and copying him, brushing off her pants, "they'd just shoot it."

He raised an eyebrow. "That's correct." He shielded his eyes with his hand and looked out ahead. "Listen. Let's make a deal about this hike. We'll eat lunch in the lowest trees we find, then head back."

"How far do you think that is?"

"Two more miles. Are you good for it?"

"This is the farthest I've ever gone."

"It's good for you. You have to get your heart rate up every day."

Two hours past noon they reached the sudden tilt in the ground that eventually rose—still another mile before them—into the distant mountains socked in by clouds. The greasewood and sage gave way to taller brush, smaller trees braceleted with poison oak and ivy. It was dense. There was no trail.

It was hot. Everything bleached white and yellow in the punishing heat. When Lamb turned and saw the girl working her legs and sweating and squinting into the sun—Christ, what can a man say? It was like his bones had been wired tight all his life, and seeing her that way, everything suddenly went slack. His mind unwinding like a spool of loose thread. What a man she rendered him, simply by being a girl who could be picked up and moved: what he wanted to be, what he ought to be, what was most unintelligible and unplanned and true in him when he carried her out of her fettered world to this. How powerful she was as long as she asserted no will of her own.

"You okay back there?" he called into the open blue before him.

"Yep."

"Strong girl."

"It's from swimming," she called up.

He stopped. "Jessie really took you swimming?"

She put her hand to her forehead. "Every morning at five in the goddamned morning. He makes me do a mile in his lane, then he does another one."

He stared at her. "Did he take you swimming on the mornings I picked you up and took you for pancakes?"

She shrugged.

"Well." He nodded. "Good for Jessie."

"Yeah," she snorted. "But not so good for me."

He turned around and increased his pace. "I am not going to have any sympathy then," he said, "knowing you can swim a mile."

When they came into the trees they were surrounded by white legs of aspen, yellow leaves flashing like golden coins above them. Sweet clover and Queen Anne's lace, cow parsnip and yarrow and stemless white flowers in pretty green-and-white whorls at their feet. Clouds came up above the

canopies of trees and the wind swept them across
a sky so simultaneously bright and dark it stopped
David Lamb's heart and he thought, this is it, this
is the limit of all of it, right here: me and this child
and all the money and progress that's brought us
here. This is the limit. And he smelled the sunblock
and his own sweat and knew that the end of the
story had already begun.

They sat cross-legged on the earth. Lamb took
off his father's ball cap—because I'm sitting down
to a meal, he said—and opened his pack and removed the potted ham and butter sandwiches and
the girl took the apple juice out of her pack.

"Oops," he said. "We forgot cups. You don't
mind sharing?"

"Nah."

"What if I have cooties?"

She rolled her eyes.

"What, you don't care?"

"I don't believe in cooties."

"That's dangerous thinking if I've ever heard it."

"Well, I'm thirsty."

A big wind moved through the bunched tops of
spruce and fir, and the long white aspen swayed like
wooden pins. The girl's hair blew across her bluish
face.

"You look like a dead girl."

"I do?"

"Your face is all white. It's a little unsettling. Did you eat that flower?"

"No."

"You look very, very strange. Your skin is iridescent."

"I wish I could see."

"Here. I have an idea." Lamb set his half-eaten sandwich on the top of his pack and ran a fingerful of dark, greenish-black dirt in three stripes across each of her cheekbones.

"Was that a cow patty?"

"Probably at some point."

"Sick, Gary."

"But it looks beautiful, Em. You look beautiful. I wish you could see."

"How does it look?"

"Like you're some wild stray piece of earth that took the form of a girl." He looked at her. "I'm going to tell you something very serious, but you have to promise not to take it the wrong way."

"Okay."

"Are you listening with all your ears?"

"Yes."

"Just this, Tommie: you will never look so beautiful again in this lifetime." He opened the apple juice and handed it to her. "Drink that." He picked up his sandwich. "I don't want you getting dehydrated. You're a great little hiker. I'm proud of you."

"Thanks." She lifted the bottle to her mouth.

"If you were in Lombard today, what would you be doing?"

"Right now?"

"Yeah."

She looked up into the tree branches. "Probably be going home from school."

"All alone?"

"I'd check my computer. Or watch TV."

"When you get back home, will you make yourself potted ham and butter sandwiches and think of me?"

"Sure." She leaned back on one hand and took a bite. "If you can get this stuff."

"You can find it at the 7-Eleven."

"I'm not supposed to go in those."

"The 7-Eleven?"

"Mom says weird people hang out there."

"That's a good mom."

"I guess."

"So I'll send you boxes of potted ham. No return address. It will be very mysterious. And when you open a can you can pretend it's a love letter."

"Gary!"

"Oh, ignore me. You should ignore everything I say."

She made like bearing her fangs when she noticed him staring at her. They finished their sandwiches and juice, and Lamb took a chocolate bar out of his pack and broke it in half.

"Know what we need to really make this perfect?"

She took half the chocolate.

"Binoculars." He nodded up toward the north end of the plain. "I bet we could see all kinds of mule deer and pronghorn."

"Those dots?"

"If we go back into town, we'll get you a pair. They're expensive."

"Like how much?"

"Hundreds. Tell you what. We get a pair, they're yours to keep."

"Okay."

"We're going to need a moving truck to get all your new stuff back to Illinois."

She laughed.

"Where are you going to hide all of your presents when you get home?"

"My closet."

"You've already figured it out."

"Yep."

"Doesn't anybody go in your closet?"

"Nope."

"Not even your mom on Saturday mornings when she's gathering the laundry."

"I do my own laundry."

"Do you really?"

"Yep."

"No, really?"

"For serious."

"Do you separate the whites and the colors?"

"Whites get hot, colors get cold."

"You're a resourceful girl, you know that?"

When they finished and packed up their things, he stood. "I'm going to see a man about a horse. You stay put." The girl waited and Lamb watched her from a distance, zipping up. When she looked up, he held up his thumbs and index fingers in a rectangle as if he were holing her in the frame of a photograph. He could see the little white flash of her smile, and when he reached her, he went into his pack and handed her a little tuft of toilet tissue. "Your turn. That man wants to know what you think of a red pony."

"Huh?"

"After you wipe, put this under a rock or use a stick to put some dirt over it."

"Gary!"

"Don't get squeamish on me. This is just our bodies, right? Don't you know how a male body works?"

"Yeah."

"Good. And I know how a female body works. Okay?'

"Okay."

"Good. I'm glad we got that out of the way. Now go on and take care of business."

They hiked in through the valley side by side, two dark figures tracing the grassy inside slope of a pale green parabola, their shadows lengthening before them, the girl in a wreck of sweat and dirt and dust and sunblock and cow shit.

They reached the shop again in late afternoon, the girl carrying the empty canteens, one over each shoulder, canvas straps marking her chest. Lamb was bare chested, his blue work shirt tied into a turban over the girl's head. He hadn't known about skin like hers. Even sunblock couldn't help. He should have spread cow shit all over her face.

"We'll help you rinse off with cool water and soap you off before it hurts to the touch."

"It doesn't feel bad."

"It will." He ran his hands under the hose faucet and back through his hair. "If we were out working we'd rinse our hats and shirts in the river and put them back on."

"Can I get a root beer?"

"Good idea. Get me one of those other beers will you?"

"Do I get a sip?"

"One sip. Take it right off the top and bring me the rest. I'll get the soap."

Lamb went into the cabin for towels and bath soap and on his way out saw a flash of Alison Foster's white hair in the doorway of the shop. In two steps Lamb was through the door, filthy, old ratty towels rolled up beneath his arm, and just in time to see Tommie—her face a terrific ruin—turning around from the workbench and lowering the open beer from her lips, her little mouth pursed in a conspiratorial grin pointed mistakenly at Foster, whose presence she'd taken for Lamb's.

Lamb stepped past the old man, took the beer from her hand, and slapped her full across the face. His hand stung and for a moment he was afraid she was going over. It was too much. He'd never hit anyone so small. She looked up at no one, stunned. She raised her hand to her face. She made no sound. He loved her for it.

"Go inside."

"I hate you." A shaking whisper.

"No you don't."

She looked from Lamb to the old man and back again and ran out. Lamb stood still, blood beating hard in the sides of his neck and inside his thighs and rushing hot through his face and the palms of his hands. It was the sun working in him. He let his eyes shut halfway and took a deep, steadying breath. She'd go off in the grass behind the shop, or beyond the outbuildings or to the river. She'd be back. There was nowhere for her to go. He set the full beer on the workbench. The breeze from the open window was cool and the blue sky was beginning to darken. Shadows were already capturing the trees at the river. Box elder leaves paler than they'd been two days ago.

Lamb exhaled. "I'm sorry you had to witness that."

"Well." Foster widened his small eyes and looked at the floor. For half a minute neither man spoke.

"She's never done that before."

"I guess a little taste of beer never hurt anybody." Lamb said nothing.

"You went for a walk," Foster said. It was not a question.

"We had a little snack out there behind some old homestead."

"Thought I saw you going north." Lamb envisioned the old man on his rooftop with binoculars.

"You shouldn't," Foster said.

"We didn't. Well, initially we did. But we crossed back and went out that way." He looked off beyond the old man as if he were pointing through the wall. "How far does that go?"

"Ninety mile."

"All BLM?"

"Mostly."

"Not much out there."

"Beef cows."

"We saw signs of that."

"You don't want to go north," Foster said again.

"Some unfriendly landowners that way, what?"

The old man watched Lamb. "Ed Granger. Had a metal plate put in his head in eighty-one."

"That right?"

"Never been right since."

"Where's that property start?"

"And he doesn't like children."

"I see."

"Maybe you ought to go see about her."

Lamb looked up. "Who? Em?"

Foster returned the gaze.

"She's okay." Lamb gestured with his head toward the cabin, wondering if Foster had seen her outside, through the window behind him. "She's got a lot to deal with right now. Her mom gone and all."

Foster looked at him with eyes Lamb couldn't read.

"Her own mother was the drunk in that wreck."

"Shame."

"I know it."

"But this is no place for a girl." The old man surveyed the steel beams crossed above them. "Helped my brother-in-law Calhoun put this place up in seventy-four."

"I remember you saying."

"He had a godchild running around here back and forth all over the goddamned place. Just about lost her arm on a square of sheet metal." He made a slicing motion across the belly of his forearm. "She was just a little thing." The old man shook his head. "Kind of picture you don't forget."

"No, I'm sure."

"Seventy-eight miles to a hospital. As you would know."

Lamb looked out the window behind him toward the river and tree line, as if he might find the correct response out there. "I didn't think things through too well, I guess. I'm not used to having a child around." He turned back to Foster. "But if that's the closest hospital, that's something I should have taken into consideration."

"You ought to take her home. Your home. Somebody's home."

Lamb said nothing.

"Pardon me if I'm speaking out of line."

"No," Lamb said, "you're right. I guess we'll head back in a couple days. I was just . . . we're expecting company. A friend."

The old man held his chin up. He raised a palsied, spotted hand. "I'll leave you to your troubles." He made for the door.

"Was there something you wanted, Foster?"

"Just see how you're getting on. Let you know snow's on its way."

"We'll be all right. You're welcome anytime."

"Pretty night coming on."

"Yeah, she is."

When the old man left, Lamb leaned against the workbench, his back to the window, and drained the beer as the shop darkened. He waited. He moved the lawn chair from beside the woodstove to the far corner of the shop and sat on the floor, his legs stretched out before him. He sat there an hour, then went out through the bunk room door and pissed in the weeds. It was dark but he could still see the green of the grass. He waited. Listened. He had no sense of where she was, so he walked back into the shop and left the door open behind him—that was as far as he'd go. She must have been waiting for it, because soon after he heard the main door swing open. She caught it to keep it from slamming, but he knew she was coming. When she stepped into the doorway the night was lit up blue-black behind her. She stood still looking in. He could tell she'd washed her face.

"You were supposed to be the lookout," he said from the floor across the room.

"I'm sorry."

"You have to pay attention to everything now. Do you see? Everything depends upon it. Our friendship depends upon it. You have to be awake."

She was crying. She'd been crying for some time. She came to him.

"Tell me what it is," he said.

She nodded and made little choking noises back in her throat. It was big crying. She ran her arm beneath her nose and Lamb reached into his pocket for a handkerchief. "Here," he said, but she let it hang loosely in her fingers and fall from her hand. He picked it up and she took it, wiped her nose. "What's the worst of it? That you feel bad like you ran away?" She shook her head. "That I slapped you?" She shrugged. "That you feel stupid. You feel like I tricked you into liking me then I turned around made you look bad in front of Mr. Foster." She nodded. "Well. That makes sense. And I'm not surprised. But I want to say something about that, okay? When you calm down. Will you sit down here beside me? I'm not going to touch you. Right here. Good. Okay." She sat on her feet a few inches beside him. "Now take a deep breath. That's not a deep breath. Come on. I'll do it with you. Ten of them, okay? Inhale," he said. "All the way, nice and slow. Let it out. Nice and slow. Again. Big deep breath. Okay. Nine. Big breath. Again." She breathed and listened to him breathe and counted backward to zero. "Better? Do you feel better?"

She shrugged.

"You're shrugging at me."

She shrugged again.

"You must be very upset."

She stared at the floor.

"Can you listen to me even though you're upset? Good. Now. Come over here. I can touch you? It's okay if I touch you? How's your skin? All burnt to hell, huh?" She smiled, and he put his arm around her and drew her in. "Come here, Tom. That's all. Good." He combed back her greasy hair with his fingers until his hand was behind her head. "Now," he said, "I know that you're upset. But what we've just done, my dear, is protect our friendship exactly the way we've been saying we'd have to. Right?" The girl did not move. He spoke very low, very gentle. "Imagine if I had not reacted like an angry uncle. What do you think Mr. Foster would have done? What do you think he would have made of a man letting his niece drink beer?"

Shrug.

"It's child abuse, Tom."

"It is?"

"Yes. It is."

"He might call the police then," she said, her voice hoarse from crying.

"Maybe. Although—and I'm not sure if this would be much better—he might just start stopping by a lot, right? Checking in. Ruining the week."

"Oh."

"But at worst, Tom, eventually he probably would have called somebody. Then I would have gone to jail, the police would have found out who you are and where you belong, and how do you think they would react to that back in Lombard?"

"Not good."

"That's correct. Not good." They looked each other in the eye. "And what do you think Mr. Foster is actually thinking now?"

She stared down at the concrete floor.

"Out here you step out of line your dad'll whip off his belt and bend you over and give you hell and high water."

"Oh."

"So I'll tell you what's happening right now down the road in that little white-painted house. Mr. Foster is mixing a basin of warm soapy water to wash his sick wife's face with, and he's thinking only about her, and about the temperature of the water, whether it's too hot or too cold, and of her wrinkled face, and of whether she knows it's him washing her. Maybe he's crying over her face. Maybe he's over crying about it. But I'll tell you one thing he isn't thinking about: you and me. Because on his walk back through the evening he would have already decided that in terms of us, everything is as right as rain. Wouldn't he?"

"Yes."

"And no police, and no angry mom, and no friends in Lombard who think you were in love with me and running away from Jessie. Right? Everything fine, the evening fine, the sky the color of a dark blue crayon, and the wind picking up because it's October, and it's the mountains, and it was all more beautiful than anything our girl had ever seen, right?"

She nodded at the floor, then looked up at him. "His wife is sick?"

"Very sick."

"Aren't you cold?"

He looked down at his chest. "No," he said. He took her hand and opened her palm and pressed it to him. "Feel how warm."

"Me too."

"I know it. You're sunburned. And Tommie, dear. Will you look at me? Can you see me?" She looked up.

"Didn't we say this was going to require being a lookout, protecting each other? Didn't we say this was unusual?"

"Yes."

"I know we did. We shook on it. And you're a girl who keeps her word." He reached for the handkerchief and wiped at her tears. "It just breaks my heart to see you crying."

This renewed her tears some.

"Say you forgive me. Say you understand."

"I forgive you. I understand."

"But do you mean it?"

"Yes," she whispered.

"Oh, Tom." He opened his arms. "Come. Will you hug me? Will you let me hug you?" He wrapped his arms around her. "You've washed up. But I'm all stinking and sweaty."

"I only washed my face," she said over his shoulder.

"I'm sorry about the cow shit."

"I don't think it was cow shit."

"Your body feels very warm. Do you think you have a fever?"

"I don't know."

"Does your body hurt?"

"A little."

"Ache from hiking or ache from fever? Can you tell?"

"I can't tell."

"Well, it's probably both." He held her thirty seconds, a minute, two minutes during which they did not speak or move. "Tom."

"Mm-hm."

"I'm not a bad guy. Do you believe me?" He put his hands to her shoulders and pushed her away a little and looked at her, holding on to her.

She nodded.

"This is something I've been keeping from you, okay? And we said we'd share everything, didn't we?"

"Yes."

He put two fingers beneath her chin and drew her face toward his own. "In Iowa we said we weren't going to do this. Do you know what I'm referring to?"

"I think."

He made a troubled face. "Tommie. I'm sort of out of familiar territory here. Do you understand?"

Nod.

"You feel a little bit the same way, don't you? Please say yes or no. Please do me that courtesy."

"Yes."

"Yes you do?"

"Yes I do."

"Do you know what I'm talking about?"

"I think so."

"You think so. Okay." He held her, her head in his hand. She sat sideways on her knees. "I don't know what to do here, Em."

"Okay."

"Okay." He laughed. "You're not going to help me, are you?"

She stared at him. He lifted her face again, close to his own. Her eyes were the largest he'd ever seen them. And here's the truest statement anywhere about her: she was the loveliest, the most perfect creature he had ever had the honor to touch beneath the face, to take up in his arms. He pressed his mouth lightly to hers—it was very small and chaste. A fatherly kiss. Then he pulled his head back a little and surveyed her face in the dark. "We said we weren't going to do that, didn't we?" His voice was raspy. His breath smelled just faintly of beer. "But we both sort of wanted to, didn't we?" She nodded, and he pulled her in and squeezed her then let go again. "Does this feel scary to you?"

Shrug.

"Does it feel like we're doing something that isn't allowed?"

"Sort of." She was barely audible.

"Because I kissed you or because I'm older than you."

Shrug.

"Don't shrug on this one, Emily Tom. We need to look at this from every angle. We need to confront it, right? Is it because you've never kissed anyone before? Or because I'm a little older than you are?"

She nodded.

"Both?"

"Both," she said.

"Good. I need to hear that. Let me tell you something about age, okay? When you get older, you begin to appreciate how short life is. I mean really short. I mean you really get to know it. Like in your bones. And what happens then, is everybody be-comes a little ageless."

"Oh."

"Does that make sense?"

"A little."

"Tell me something. Doesn't Jessie ever kiss you good night?"

"No."

"And no uncles? No grandfathers?"

"No."

"So this would seem a little odd, wouldn't it? Even though it's a normal expression of affection."

Nod.

"Do you think it doesn't feel good to give you a kiss like that?"

No response.

"Let me say that another way. Do you think I'm trying to hurt you?"

"No."

"Good. Because I'm not. Do you believe me?"

"Yes."

"Sometimes when men and women kiss and are . . . you know, like that with each other. Some-times people get their hearts broken, right? People sometimes get hurt. That's how it's said. Right?" He held her close. She was like a little furnace. He drew her up onto his lap. "Maybe that's what hap-pened to Sid? Or to your mom, right?"

"When Sid's cousin broke up with her boyfriend, she cut up her arms with a fork."

Lamb made a face. "Because her heart was broken?"

"I think so."

"Oh, Em. Promise me you'll never do anything like that."

"I would never."

"I know you wouldn't. You love life too much. It's partly that love of life that I saw in you that day in the parking lot."

"I know."

"You do?"

"Yeah."

"Good. And I want you to know there are ways we can keep our hearts safe. There are ways we can keep your heart from breaking, and mine."

"There are?"

He laughed a little in the dark. "Of course there are. And that's exactly what we're doing by talking about this. And that's exactly what we'll continue to do. Do you understand?" He looked down at her.

"You will. I promise. When you're twenty and I'm dead and gone and you look back on this night, you are not going to feel heartbroken. Okay?"

"Okay."

"Do you want to put your head in my lap and just sit here a little while?"

"Okay."

"Here you go. Let's just sit here a minute like this. And look down at your face and see if you look like you have a fever. We're not going to sleep on this hard floor. We're just resting together."

"I'm comfortable."

"You're comfortable. No you are not." He moved his fingers in small circles in her hair, in her scalp.

"That feels good."

"I know it does. Was it a pretty night out there?"

"I was too sad."

"Was it even more sad because the night was pretty?"

"Yes."

"My heart is just like yours. Did you know that?"

"It is?"

"It is."

"That's how we knew to go back to the parking lot."

"That's right." He laughed. "That's right." They lay still. "Em?"

"Yeah."

"Do you want to rest on the bottom bunk awhile? And I can check you for a fever until morning? This floor is killing my old bones."

She pressed the back of her head against his blue jeans, looking at him, and he lifted her onto his knee and pulled her up. She leaned her head against his shoulder. He kissed the cheek, and kissed the jaw, and kissed her mouth. "Okay?"

She nodded.

He stood up, still holding her, supporting her bottom on his hip and arm. She draped her arms around his neck like a child. He took her into the little bunk room. "Do you want some cool water?" He felt her shrug. "Are you just going to shrug now all the time?"

"Maybe I am."

"Stubborn girl."

She shrugged again. And our guy told her it would be his understanding, from here on out, that whenever she shrugged, it would mean she was saying how much she liked him. It would be her way of saying yes.

He set her down. "Are you too warm in those clothes?"

She looked down at her blue jeans and shirt. "Not too."

"We should at least take off our socks. So we don't inadvertently plant a grasslands in the sheets. Careful. Those little seeds are sharp."

They sat beside each other on the bottom bunk and removed their socks. He laid them neatly over the back of the metal chair. "Good," he said. "Can you stand a minute? I'd like to turn down the bed for you, dear." He pulled back the blanket and sheet, folding the wool blanket into quarters at the end of the bed, unzipped his sleeping bag wide and laid it over the top, then held it all open for her. "Go on," he said. "Climb in."

When they were both in, he pulled her up so her head was on his shoulder, her tiny arm over the great barrel of his chest, and he turned his head down a little to see her face.

"Em. Does this remind you of anything? A movie? A TV show?"

"What?"

"This. Now. This little house, and the shop, and you and me in it, and nothing else around. The things we're sharing. Did you ever see a TV show like this or a movie or something?"

"I don't think so."

"Think hard."

"I am."

"Think of all the movies and songs and books you know. Are any of them like this?"

"No."

"You're sure? Double sure?"

"Double sure."

"Isn't that good news?"

"I guess."

"Remember when we said if we went back far enough in time, the planet would be flooded with seawater, and we'd have to reinvent the world from scratch?"

"Yeah."

"Remember we said this time, we'd get it right?"

"I remember."

"That was just pretend, right? But Em"—he lowered his voice to a whisper—"I think we're really doing it. Because no one's ever had this before. Do you understand? No one gets to have this, what we're having. No one ever has. We're inventing it."

"Gary."

"Yeah."

"What day is it?"

"A Thursday."

"What day in October?"

"Do you want to say two more days? We'll stay two more days?"

"Okay."

"We can revise as we go."

"Okay."

"You're such an empathetic little body."

She looked up at him.

"It means you're good at imagining how other people are feeling."

"Oh."

"I wish I could give you this and home with your mother at the same time."

"Me too."

"I'll try to think of a way."

"For both?"

"You trust me, don't you?"

"Yes."

"I know you do."

They were both up in the night, the girl with a fever, her face burning, Lamb filling her canteen and holding her head and tipping it into her mouth and feeding her broken aspirin. Helping her up and opening the little metal side door so she could piss outside in the dirt. They did not sleep when she was burning up and her clothes hurt her skin and her bones were cold and then her bones were hot and it hurt to breathe. Her eyes were burnt, she said, and dirt was stuck to the insides of her eyelids.

"Sunglasses," he said. "I should have bought you sunglasses."

He laid the edge of his hand at the hip of her jeans, his head filled with fire. Dark early morning hour. No crickets, no coyotes, no sound but their breath, their whispering, as if even here they did not want to be overheard.

"Is it better or worse?"

"Better."

"Should we fold back the blankets?"

"Please."

He climbed out of bed and rolled everything back to the metal frame at the end.

"When's the last time anyone held you like this? Or was beside you in bed like this?"

"That day."

"What day?"

"That day you threw me in your truck."

"Did I throw you?"

"I hit my head."

"I'm sorry, Em. Do you forgive me?"

"I forgive you."

"Who held you then?"

"Mom. When she got home from work."

"Tell me how it was."

"I was in bed already."

"What time was it?"

Shrug.

"No, Em. You have to tell me exactly how it was." He pushed her by the shoulders a little away from him and looked at her. "Look at my face and tell me the story."

"It was six or something."

"Still light out?"

"Yes."

"You were upset. I'd upset you. Say it. Say: you upset me, Gary."

"You did."

"That's good for me to hear. Tell me. Mom was worried about you? She thought you were sick?"

"I guess."

"What did she say?"

"She asked if I was sick and I said a little."

"And she sat on the edge of the bed with you?"

"She brought us a snack in bed."

"What snack?"

"Milk and strawberry toast."

"That's a good snack."

"I know."

"And she gave you the snack and went off with Jessie?"

"She stayed with me."

"For a little while?"

"For the whole night."

"What did Jessie do?"

"TV I guess."

"You were crying in bed?"

"Yes."

"Because I'd scared you."

"And because my friends. They wouldn't answer when I called. Their moms said they weren't home. But I knew they were."

"You were shaken up."

"I don't know."

"But you came to find me the next day?"

"Yes."

"Why?"

"I don't know."

"I thought things weren't so good in that apartment."

"Sometimes they were."

Picture the black dawn. The spray of stars overhead. Alison Foster, poor old son of a bitch, limping
back up the dirt drive of the old Calhoun place with
his red Maglite, gray head trembling, eyes impossibly small and hard and squinting ahead as if he
could see David Lamb and the child in the dark. As
if he knew. As if he'd catch them at it. As if Lamb
didn't know Foster was out there prowling around
and peering in the cabin windows. Thinking what?

Foster didn't get it that when Lamb drives her in
his truck off the paved roads and into a place bright
and stark and sere, beyond the humid Midwestern
acres of hog feed and furrowed till, the girl—his
girl, Lamb's girl—is perfectly okay. Foster didn't
get that it's a favor, a gift, say, taking her beyond
the miserable reaches of prairie restoration reeking
of sewage processing plants and cornstarch facto-
ries. That she rode along in the passenger seat with
her eyes half closed and fixed upon Lamb as though
he were the handsomest, wisest, most beneficent
man on planet Earth.

Besides, Foster wouldn't have found them in the
cabin. Runny moonlight cast long, bent shadows
across the concrete floor of the bunk room, though
Lamb had tried to cover the windows with squares
of a stiff and mildewed drop cloth he found folded

beneath the workbench. Faint smell of woodsmoke, fire snapping in the iron stove. Outside the shop the north fork of the river running black past a stand of narrow-leafed cottonwoods just beyond the county road. A spectral mist hung rib-high among the water birch along its banks. A single box elder clenched its branches against the cold.

And his girl was sleeping beside him, her wonderful blue-and-white flowered nightgown twisted up around her bare, freckled waist. Soft belly rising a little with each breath, her warm damp head resting on Lamb's outstretched arm, sweat shining at her temples, her mouth open, her little lips open—Christ, she was small—and he was swearing mutely into the space above him that this was good for her. That as long as he was honest and approached this thing from every possible angle, everything would line up and fall into place of its own accord, like atoms helixed and pleated tight within the seeds of cheatgrass needling the hems of her tiny blue jeans: fragile, inevitable, life-giving, and bigger than he. Such was his faith in the forces that had given rise to the girl herself, to the rapid trills of violet green swallows up the mountain, to the spoon-shaped leaves of prairie buttercups they'd seen blanketing the roadside in eastern Wyoming.

Lamb was just a man in the world. He'd fed her well and told her stories and loved her up all the way through the dim-lit outskirts of Rockford, Iowa City, Omaha; across the national grasslands, stiff and pale in the increasing cold; over the continental divide as the sky shed itself in falling snow, and up to where there were no trees, no birds, no life but the slow force of rock rising up from a thin and frozen crust of ground. Say this was all in hopes of glimpsing something beautiful. And is there anything wrong with that?

The next morning was just like all of their mornings: three little silver pans going at the tapered end of Tommie's trapper fire. Coffee and canned meat and beans and toast with jam and four eggs.

"There. Now tomorrow your fire will be even better."

She pulled her lips into her mouth and lifted her little face up at him. "It's working, though."

"You won't forget how to do it, will you?"

"Nope."

"Should I send you little reminder notes? With directions and diagrams?"

She made a face.

"It'll give you dreams of the next man you're going to build a trapper fire with. Only this guy, you'll have to teach *him* how to do it." He lifted his chin and turned his face away. "It hurts my feelings to say that, Tom. But we have to say it."

She stirred the beans. "Nope," she said. "Only building a fire with you. Cross my heart and hope to die."

"Don't say that, Em. Someday you'll get married and you'll go camping with your husband, and he won't know how to build a fire. You'll have to show him what I taught you."

"I won't get married."

"Won't you work for the forest service when you're out of college? And tell me how to find you so I can come visit you in your tent? I'll be that old camper who's always haunting the high plains, right? I'll wear an orange cap so you'll know me. Even from far away." He bent over and kissed the crown of her head. "I want you to always remember that I never let you eat a meal out here that was something we added hot water to."

"Like oatmeal, puke."

"Or dehydrated vegetables. I want you to remember all the meals we made together, and how every one of them had whole beans it. What's happening underneath that toast?"

She tipped her head sideways and checked the smoke, checked the flames, and looked up at him.

"Go ahead. Let me see you fix that."

With a white branch she rearranged the logs to keep the natural windbreak from burning it up too quickly, then turned to the little pile of sticks and tree punk and pine needles and twigs and pushed a handful in beneath the lowermost level of burning wood.

"If you're ever alone in the woods waiting for me," he said, "you'd be okay. Wouldn't you?"

"Yep."

"You'd know how to make it through the night."

"Yep."

She placed the white branch behind her in the cold grass.

"You've learned a thing or two about being an outdoorswoman."

"I know."

After eating and rinsing the pans, Lamb would drink his second cup of coffee and they'd walk up the hill across the spans of sagebrush and sumac and along a deep empty draw. Rust-bitten iron and steel lay in broken pieces in the weeds—comb of a hay rake, the axle and wheels of a mowing machine. They'd pass it on their way to the same grassy promontory each morning from where Lamb would point to the distant foothills, the innermost point, he told her, of a spiral of mountain and rock, like a granite wall corkscrewed around the little mountain lair she'd inherit—he promised—when he died.

If we were going to stay out here, he told her, we'd set up this little coal-burning stove, polish it till it turned black again, and we'd bring a little life back to this place. Then we'd build a new stable of blond wood, and I'd buy you a string of ponies. You could learn all the old ways. Boiling pudding in a bag. Decorating caraway seed cakes with burnt sugar. Trapping and roasting prairie chickens. We'd get some hired help, nice young guys from Idaho or Oregon who could put up a new rail fence around front and keep all the fences mended.

We'd bring it all back. You'd pack us lunches in metal lard buckets we'd hang from our saddles, and you'd sneak the best things into my pail, wouldn't you? A thick layer of butter on my ham sandwich. By day you'd boil my shirts and hang them to dry outside. And when we got back at the end of the day and scrubbed our faces and hands with gritty soap, we'd line up at our long wooden kitchen table, you at the head in a flowered dress, passing down all the warm dishes of food. When it's all set out upon the table, we'll all bow our heads, and I'll say the blessing, right? In the winter when it's just you and me by the fire, we'll commit whole chapters of the Bible to memory, so I'll really be prepared. And do you know who will be the first person I pray for? Your mother.

And Christ he wanted to freeze her in time on the mountain, her tangled hair the color of pale tree bark, her burnt skin peeling off her face in bluish flakes, and he'd lie down with her there in the magnificently bright light, beside her on the bittercress and weeds, the old rusted hay rake beside them, angry red-winged blackbirds wheeling in great dark hoops above them.

We're all alone out here, he would say. Is the sky bright, or what? Listen to those mad birds. We're reinventing the world, my dear. Here. Yes. Like that. Are you comfortable? Isn't this nice? Do you know how lucky we are to have this?

He stared at her little heart-shaped face and kissed her cheek and kissed her mouth and a thrilling horror spread like a stain through the hollow of his chest.

"We can't help it, can we?" he whispered hoarsely. He opened his hand over her heart and held her there. "This was too big for us. It was too big for us it swallowed us up didn't it?"

Shrug.

"Oh, you sweet child. Do that again."

Shrug. She shut her eyes.

"Just hold my hand, okay? And we'll sleep. Just as we are, just like this. Just a nap out in the wind and light. Yes. We're not taking this any farther. Just this. Thank you."

In a little while, he lifted her up out of the grass and carried her down the hill and back inside and tucked her into bed beside him.

· · · · ·

The woodstove snapped and hissed and a thin wind sang again across the chimney pipe, racing high, chasing nothing. Tommie lay her head sideways upon David Lamb's chest, her knees pressed against either side of his ribs, her ear against his heart, like a wet little chorus frog pressed against him for heat, and she asked him what he was like when he was a boy, when he was little, and then her age, and he told her to shush, to close her eyes.

Imagine a whole canvas of pale greens waving and strung with bees and all about you the music of swallows and sparrows and shrikes. And there in the middle of it is our Lamb, a boy, big eyed with ironed Levi's and clean short hair and he's the only one of all four boys his mother kissed before he left the house in the morning. In his pocket, two dimes she gave him and only him and he'll add them to his pile of dimes and steal the black taffy and Long Boys and Atomic FireBalls from Bonn Drugg's and share them magnanimously with all the fellows. For now he is walking through this grass, skimming his open palms across their feathered and green-needled tops wondering what he will buy when he has a hundred dollars. And the answer is absolutely whatever he wants. What a joy to be alive in the world as the tallest boy with the broadest shoulders and a pile of dimes in your closet and as many candy bars as you can stuff in your pockets day after day after day.

Somewhere behind him the boys are laughing, a dozen of them making a baseball diamond in the cinders on the street. A cork ball. A single wooden bat. He could play but then no one else would have a chance to make the best hit or the best catch or pitch and he is tearing up the Queen Anne's lace because it looks like his mother's stupid doilies she's always needling with alone up in her room with the door shut. He tears them up, every single lacy white flower with his fists as he walks, and he throws them all shredded across the top of the stupid fucking grass because the last thing the world needs is another doily.

The sound of a train lumbers and clanks over the metal tracks on the far side of the meadow. In his back pocket he carries a torn page from a Superman comic that wasn't his, but should have been his, and a pocketknife of his father's that he's not supposed to touch, that he'd been belt-whipped once already for touching when he carved his name in the cedar mantelpiece. In the torn-out picture, Superman is diving and swooping over a train and all the women in the windows are looking up at him, the men just go on reading their newspapers—they don't even know what's happening—and the train is called TRIUMPH in golden letters and Superman can fly above it in figure eights and lift the whole thing off the tracks and over his head, which he doesn't do in the picture David stole, but which David Lamb knows he could do. Knows it.

Mornings before Mom's car wreck, Glenn comes over from next door knocking on the back door in the morning and singing out Ole Davy! Ole Davy! Lamb's father curses and Glenn tells him good morning Mr. Lamb and Davy's not allowed out till he's finished his breakfast. Within ten minutes there is a chorus of boys outside the back door calling out with Glenn, everybody calling his name, everybody waiting for Davy in order to start the day, and his mother ushers him outside and tells him go save the day, Davy—a little song she sings every summer morning. And she gives him one of her paper-wrapped raisin biscuits she keeps just for herself in a tin above the stove and kisses the crown of his shining head. Neither Henry nor Mark leaves the table because there's no one out there who even wants to see either of them. Nobody ever wants to see any of them except Davy.

But every morning before his mother's wreck, David's littlest brother run outs behind him calling Davy, Davy wait. Davy wait. Crying out. Running, tripping, falling, every morning a fucking embarrassment. Broken tooth one day, scraped-up face the next day, blood and snot and crying all over the place yelling wait wait Davy. But he won't ever catch up and won't ever get a raisin biscuit or two dimes or know a thing about Superman. How could he? He's Nel.

Ten years later and it seems everywhere in town is the smell of soft tar and petrol and the distant crash of breaking glass and screaming tires and Les Brown and Doris Day singing out the bedroom window of his skirt-chasing father.

Every day as a young man David wears a clean, starched button-down shirt. When he drives he keeps his hands at ten and two, and he'll take the car straight across the fallow fields, off the road, a cold beer or two or three on the floor of the passenger seat. He is the only one his mother bought a car for, and now that she is gone he takes it wherever he wants. And why shouldn't he? He'll never get a dime from his father, no matter that Henry and Mark left them all to rot there, including Dad. No matter that Dad wouldn't eat if it weren't for David, wouldn't have clean clothes, would probably be arrested because

Nel never goes to school, instead he mopes and reads books alone and sleeps behind the Texaco. Won't even sleep in the house anymore.

When she buys him the car it is almost new and now the chassis is already half eaten with rust from driving over creeks and down creeks and the rotors are warping, he can hear it.

Next thing, Nel disappears. One night like every night he goes to sleep behind the Texaco and in the morning he is gone. No one knows where he's gone and no one is looking and no one cares. Wherever he goes that night, he disappears, fifteen years old, and no Lamb ever sees him or hears from again.

Cathy comes to David and pulls him out of the empty house and she sets him down at her own kitchen table with a beer and a pot roast sandwich and in all the world she has chosen him.

Someone's hand between his shoulder blades. A pressed suit. A garden rake. A metal desk before him. Phones are ringing and he is looking for his little brother. Something bites every vertebra in his spine and forces his eyes down and fixes his gaze on what has suddenly become fat white concrete at his feet.

No voices. No birds. No Glenn or group of boys or even Nel. Asphalt rising up in a fixed plane in every direction. He's in a parking lot. Chicago. In a Mercedes. With his father, now dead. And every stranger's face is his own face: empty, haggard, sick of driving, sick of eating. And he will witness everything good and decent in this world humiliated and destroyed and that is just how it is. If anybody knows it, David Lamb knows it.

There is a small person inside of him wishing to tell Tommie all about it and then another person inside of him crushing the wishes like empty beer cans against a cinder-block wall. Lamb isn't stupid. He knows how the story ends. He knows that he'll keep his promise—it's the only thing he gets to keep. He'll return her to the parking lot after Linnie's come and gone. Bring her right back to where he found her. And when she walks away and looks back in his direction in a year, or two years, or three years, if she looks back at all, she will hate him. But he will have saved her. He will seal her up in silver light and deliver her back to her mother. Back into the arms of her mother.

And he will sit there in his truck, both hands on the wheel, smiling with all of his teeth, watching her go. And the wind will be dirty in his hair, and there will be no decent place left in his heart because in all this chasing nothing he will have scrubbed it out, scrubbed it hollow, and nothing can fill it back up but words he makes as beautiful as he can. A sentence that will carry, he hopes, as if it were the wind, as if there were seeds of rush and blue-eyed grass upon it. As if the alphabet could reset his bones, or restart his life.

He ran his big hands up into her thin tangled hair, careful not to pull any knots. He kissed the top of her pale head again.

"You know exactly what it's like to be me," he said. "Don't you? Don't you see me?"

She nodded into his chest.

"That's right. You do. You're my twin. Your heart is hewn to mine. Isn't it. Don't you see?"

In the night she woke to the sound of his crying. It was big crying. His face ugly and pink with it and one hand on the top of her head and the other on her hip, his chest bare, wrinkled, and finely furred, faintly gray, and the skin beginning to loosen from the bone just beneath the arms and on his forearms and the backs of his hands. She turned to face him. I've hurt you, he was saying, I have I have. Am I ruining your life? Tell me I'm not ruining your life.

She touched the back of his head, his coarse hair, and he caught it in his own and pressed it to his mouth. That such kindness should be in this world, and he its recipient.

But she said nothing, and he had never been so sorry for anything in his life. By force of will he turned his gross crying into laughing. "Oh, I'm sorry. I'm sorry. Big ugly man crying. I must be scaring you." Outside the window, he knew, behind the towels and drop cloth, Alison Foster stood shivering in a thin blue veil of falling snow. Taking notes.

"It's okay," the girl said. "I'm okay. See?"

He lifted his head and looked at her, looked at her from hairline to the dirty ends of her fingers. "You are, aren't you? You're perfectly whole." He took her in his arms and held her, rushing his hands up and down her legs and arms and shoulders and head.

When she was asleep again, he went out after Foster. He circled the shop, the cabin. Brought his own Maglite to the ruined outbuildings and checked inside. Walked to the river and looked among the trees. Up the road with his light looking for footprints in the world's thinnest gauze of snow. Up to the Fosters' house again, as he had every night, and he saw the old woman breathing mechanically in her hospital bed in the orange lamplight, and he circled the house and looked in the window of the empty bedroom, and around to the back and into the room where Foster slept in the flashing blue TV light.

In the morning the sky was bright as polished silver. Snow covered Lamb's boots and piled up to his ankles. To the north the clouds ended, a bright blue line of daylight searing as if just beneath the cloud cover—a trick of distance.

He stooped in his boots at the end of the drive, near the fence, and checked around him. There was no one watching, was there? No one who could see and remember this or report any of it, and he vomited into the snow. When he stood he kicked snow over it and went out to the street.

He checked the snow for Foster's footprints, but most of the snow had fallen after midnight. Alone in his heavy sheepskin jacket he shaved at the river, rinsed his mouth with the ice-cold water, then moved inside where he tidied the cabin and the shop, cleared it of her dirty socks, a hair rubberband, the little yellow sweater. He brought everything from the car that would not be his and stacked it all in the bunk room and stood and watched her sleeping. He returned to the cabin and brought out ratty towels and set them with the duct tape in the bunk room for extra window insulation.

"Are you packing?" The girl sat, cheeks flushed with sleep.

"No, dear. I'm just tidying up for the guests."

"What guests?"

"Shouldn't we have some? A dinner party around the fire?"

"You're insane."

"Ssh." He sat on the edge of the bed and pulled a hat over her head. "I haven't built a fire yet. It's cold. You look beautiful all drowsy and with your faced mushed with sleep."

"Did it snow?"

"Did it ever. It'll be gone by lunch."

"Oh."

"You want to go out and see?" He put his face into her hair. It smelled the way it does when it's cold outside—when there's snow. Metallic, fibrous. "Are you warm?" He held her face in his hands. "You see me now, don't you?"

"Yes."

"You know me, don't you?"

She nodded.

"I'm not embarrassed."

She shook her head. "Me either."

"I really like you."

"I like you too."

"We're lucky aren't we?"

Nod.

"Equal partners, right?"

Tommie and Lamb were out behind the cabin halfway to the hay rake and investigating a giant bear
shit covered with fur when the white car came slowly
rolling over the pockmarked road. She saw it first.

"Hey," she said and pointed. "The dinner guests."

Lamb looked up, squinted across the distance.
He turned back to the girl. "Inside." He took her
under the arm and started down the slope to the
cabin door.

"Who is it?"

"I don't know." He opened the door and took a
moment to look out to the road as he shoved the
girl inside.

His armpits and groin broke out in sweat. He
pushed her forward and she kept looking back at
him and finally they twisted and stumbled into the
cabin and he got the closet door open. The white
car turned into the dirt drive and he put Tommie
into the closet. Just lifted her by the shoulders and
set her in the closet. "This is it, Tom. This is our
first big test. Foster was nothing compared to this
okay? You good for it?"

"Who is it?"

"Do you understand the kind of trouble we'll
be in if this person sees you even once?" He held

the closet door open two inches and talked into it. "Don't make a sound. Oh, Em, I'm so sorry. It might be awhile in there." Outside, the engine of the car stopped. Tommie sat down on a pile of old boots and a fishing net and a big white cement bucket. "Who is it, Gary?"

"I think it's an old friend, Tom. You have to give me your word. Are you good for this?" She stared up at him from the floor. "This is a gift to us. If she comes and goes without seeing you, I will never get in trouble, right?"

"How did she know you were here?"

"I made a mistake, Tom. I made a miscalculation. You might hear some hard things. Tell me you love me and you'll be patient and breathe like I taught you." Last thing he saw were her eyes, rounder than ever, her little head nodding in the dark. He shut the closet, heard it latch, and went to the front door, and here she comes across the dying, splintery lawn and through the October morning calling out his name: David.

He met her in the cold sunlight and quieted her mouth with his. Took her around the waist, took a long drink of her hair pouring like liquid night down the back of her smooth green jacket, took her bag.

"You came all the way out here for me, didn't you?" He spoke into her mouth.

She pressed her smile against his.

"You drove through the night?"

"Mm-hm." She looked up at him. "Hey. What's the matter?" She looked behind him to the cabin door. She put a hand to his forehead, to his cheek. "Are you okay?"

"I saw you." He pointed up at the ridge where he and the girl had been headed. "I ran all the way down."

She just smiled at that.

"You must be exhausted." He opened the cabin door. "Here," he said, put his hand on her bottom as she stepped inside.

"Oh, David. I didn't think I was going to see this place again."

He quieted her mouth with his. "Know something? Neither did I," he whispered. She looked up at him, her face blank. "I thought I was through with you. I thought I'd gotten all the good out of you a man could get."

"You're panting."

"Well, I'm old. What," he said. "You smile. But you ought to know by now how much I actually despise you." He turned her around, guided her to the couch. "I mean really loathe you." He sat her down. "I would bet," he whispered, pressing her lengthwise into the dusty plaid upholstery, "that you want me to show you how much I hate you."

"You're not going to have a heart attack on me, are you?"

"Oh, shut up." She moved to respond and he put his finger to her lips. "No talking now," he said and drove his hand up into her hair. "I said shut up."

When the sound of tap water rushing through the pipes filled the walls, Lamb opened the closet door. The girl was hugging herself in the dark, her face wet with tears, the end of her sleeve wet and snotty. He held it open just a crack and whispered when he spoke. "Good girl," he said. "It's okay. We were just talking out here. Did you hear us talking?"

She shook her head.

"You're not the kind of girl who would say that and keep everything she'd heard to herself, are you?"

She shook her head.

They looked each other in the eye, and for one long moment neither spoke.

"It's an old friend," he said. "An old girlfriend, right? I'm going to get you out of here, okay? I'm going to open the door one more time in five minutes. You need to be good for this. Are you good for this?" She nodded. "That's my girl. I'll explain when she goes, okay? I love you. You and you alone,

Emily Tom. She is not staying long, right?" The toilet flushed. "When I open the door again, count to twenty. After twenty seconds, run straight to the shop. Quiet as a mouse."

Nod.

"You sit tight in there till I come out. You're angry with me right now. You're confused. But you trust me. You're going to be cool, calm, and collected until we talk, right? And then you can give me another black eye if you want to."

"Okay."

"Am I making the wrong decision trusting you out there? That's my girl. Good." He kissed his fingers and bent and touched them to her uplifted mouth and closed the door.

In the shop she stood still hugging herself in the dark. She looked around, then walked uncertainly into the bunk room, looking back as she stepped forward. She undressed, pulled on her nightgown and long johns, and put herself in the top bunk. In a minute she sat up, climbed back down, picked up her toothbrush, and put her feet into her slippers. She lifted her fleece off the little metal chair beside the beds, pulled it over her head, and slipped out the back door and ran across the dead broken grass to the dirt road. The Fosters. She could go there.

She stood out on the road and looked west toward the hook where Foster's little white house blinked in the cold. Then hugging herself again, she turned back to the shop and returned to her little bunk.

. . . . .

In the cabin, Lamb shut and locked the door and said a silent prayer to his old luck and took Linnie back to the couch.

"David." She took a plaid-covered end pillow and stuffed it between them. He looked at it. "Can we talk now?"

"I want to talk first. Did you want to talk first?"

"What's with you?"

"What's with me?"

"Can you relax? Is something wrong?"

"I didn't really think you'd come, Linnie."

"You didn't?"

"The truth is, I was so lonely I invited out ten or twelve women, and I've got one hidden in every room out here, and then you came along, and I'm now out of space."

"You didn't invite anyone else, did you?"

"My dear, we've never been operating on a basis of exclusivity."

"I hate you."

"And I hate you. Good. Glad we've got that all clearly drawn."

"David."

"Can we have a serious talk now?"

"I'm sorry."

"I want to say this, Linnie, okay? Seeing you come across the grass for me—it's the best thing this old guy's seen in a lifetime."

"David."

"No. Let me say this. I know there's a lot of stuff from my previous life that's been crowding you out. I know that. My previous life isn't even my previous life. Do you understand?"

"How long ago did you move out?"

"A long time. Two months. Three. I don't know."

"Why didn't you tell me?"

He looked down at his hands.

"Was it because of me?"

"Linnie, you need to not think of it that way. Listen. I'm going to tell you something that is absolutely true, okay?"

"Okay."

"Cathy knows nothing about you."

"Okay."

"People live together. They tolerate each other until they realize they've been tolerating each other, right? Sometimes it's like sleepwalking."

"She won't tolerate you having affairs."

"If there's something you want to ask, Linnie, you'd better just ask it."

"I'm sorry."

"There isn't anybody else out here. Do you see anybody out here other than you? Do you think I really called a bunch of women and invited them out, just hoping one of them would come?"

"I'm sorry."

He looked out the window over the door at the empty road, the huge curtain of blue sky above it. "Do you have the sense I'm out here getting my kicks while I'm counting the empty columns of my life?"

"Please, David. I'm sorry, okay?"

"And it's not that simple. There are things about her too. But understand it's very difficult to speak ill of her."

"I respect you the more for it."

"I know you do." He put his hands in his lap and turned to face her. "You know me, don't you."

"Sometimes."

"Linnie. Look at me. Let's have this. I want to try for it. But I'd feel like I was stealing you from the world. You're so young. You have a life to live."

"I could just wait for you. I'm willing to do that."

"I think I knew you would say that."

"Why does it make you look like you want to die? You need to not look at me like that."

He looked down at his open hands. "I'm afraid I made you say it."

"Of course you didn't."

"I'm afraid I make everybody say everything."

"You're not that powerful."

He nodded and looked at his hands.

"What about Cathy?" she asked.

"What about her."

"You make her say everything?"

"No."

"What if I say I'm not going to see you again after this?"

"I'd worry that you were trying to convince me I hadn't made you say everything up till then."

"I see the problem."

"I need a little of this space to do some soul searching, Linnie. I need to test myself. Or. Clean out my heart, you know? It's like a crowded old garage. It needs emptying and sorting."

"I don't know if you can tidy a heart like you can clean a garage, David."

"I need to try. I need to see if there's anything there."

"I used to find all this stuff in my parents' garage. Horseshoes and old mitts and notepads and hammers of solid metal. Do you know the kind I mean?"

"I know the kind."

"If you find something like that, don't throw it away."

"Aren't you even a little angry with me, Linnie?"

"Do you want me to be?"

"I think I want someone to be."

"Well, I don't want to be angry. You can't go around trying to make people angry just so you know where you stand."

"You're a smart girl."

"Maybe."

"I think I might be an awful person, Linnie."

"David, you're a decent man. Okay?"

His eyes filled. He took her face in his hands. "How do you know exactly what to say?" Linnie took his hands and he let go her face. "I'm afraid everyone's in on something really wonderful, Linnie, and I don't know what it is, and I can't be in on it."

"You're okay."

"I'm outside the window."

"No you're not."

"You'll be waiting for me, won't you?"

"I will."

"You can't help it, can you?"

"Of course I can."

"Oh, thank you for saying that." She moved the pillow and he took her up in his arms. "Are you my girl?"

. . . . .

Glacial winds blasted the mountains all night and in the morning it was bright and bitter cold. Lamb filled the woodstove and set a pan of water to boil on top while outside he built the breakfast fire for Linnie. She was bundled up in Lamb's extra clothes and wrapped in a rug, two rag-wooled hands around a tin cup of champagne. Lamb was back and forth in his sheepskin coat between the fire and the girl, the stove and the woman. He walked slowly through the wind in the space between the cabin door and the shop door and he no longer wanted to enter either room. He wanted again to lie down, this time in the snow, and see who came for him or where else they might put him.

"Why do you look so beaten up. Is it me?"

"I'm just tired, Lin. So tired."

"This is because you're feeding a dozen women breakfast, isn't it?" She winked.

Lamb raised his eyes at her, his head lowered to his cup of hot tea and whiskey. "You have no idea."

"Who's your favorite?"

He sipped from the cup. "Emily."

"Where'd you meet her?"

"I took her from a swing set in her mother's backyard."

"Yuck, David."

"She's a sweet kid. That's all. Maybe I wish I'd had a kid."

"What's so sweet about her?"

"She has freckles." He poured more whiskey into his own cup, raised to her, and she drained the champagne and held out her own cup.

"I have freckles."

"Those? Those are not freckles. Those are beauty marks."

"I thought that was supposed to be a good thing."

"Beauty marks don't need my love. Freckles need my love. Enough beans?"

"Enough for two of me."

"Enough bacon?"

"Let's go inside."

"You go ahead. I'll get these plates rinsed off so they're clean for lunch. I have a Scrabble board in the cabin somewhere. Get it out for us?"

"Can't I see the shop?"

He nodded and stood slowly. "Come on. Let's be quick and get it over with. I want to get back in bed."

The shop was warm and they carried the cold in on their coats and in their hair. Linnie had the champagne under her arm. She hopped up on the workbench and looked out the window to the road and the line of trees, blackened by the brightness of the morning sky behind them. "But it's so warm in here." She turned back to Lamb. "Why didn't we eat in here? It's cleaner than the cabin."

"A workspace has to be clean."

"Do you work out here?"

"I will. I haven't but I will."

"What are you going to do?"

"I'm going to fix up the cabin, for one. Gutter in the back is hanging off the roof. Some of the window frame needs mending." He opened the stove door to turn the wood. "The whole thing needs a good cleaning."

"That little window in the bathroom is cracked."

"I know it."

"It could clean up pretty well. You could rent it out. Like a summer cabin."

"Or I could just live in it."

"You'd get restless."

He looked out the window behind her head. "You begin to feel a lot differently about a word like restless when you're my age."

"You talk like you're infirm." She lifted the bottle. "Want to make a nest by the woodstove?"

"Out here?"

"It's great."

He nodded. "Okay, Lin. I'll get some more wood and build the fire. You go get the blankets off the couch. Let's get that rug too. Get the Scrabble board."

In the bunk room Tommie was wide awake, hands folded behind her head and just peeking out of a pile of sleeping bags.

"You're eavesdropping," he said as he closed the door behind him and approached the bed. She scrunched up her face. "We're going to sit in here for a while, okay? Are you good for it?"

"Okay."

"It's just two days she's here. Counting today."

"Okay."

"If you have to go to the bathroom, you have to be really really quiet, right?"

"I know."

"I don't have any books or anything for you. You're not going to sneak out and go back to Foster's, are you? Call Fox News and *USA Today*?"

"I'm scared."

"You'll hibernate, right? You'll be my little mountain critter hibernating in her nest all day, won't you? And when she leaves you'll be full of energy."

Hearing Linnie's footsteps, Lamb moved toward the door. Linnie turned the knob and peeked in.

"What a cool little room!"

"It's the bunk room."

"Why don't we sleep in here?"

"It gets really cold in winter."

"Can we use those blankets?"

"I was just checking them out. Smells like mice got into them."

"Too bad. We could've used them for a mattress. Or even stayed in here. Do those beds come apart?"

"Too far from the fire. Besides"—he raised an eyebrow—"it's haunted."

She took his arm. "By who?"

"There's an old man who lives up the road?"

She nodded.

"He's seventy-something, eighty. His wife had a stroke some years ago and she's there in a bed—like in-home care, right? Like a breathing corpse. It's the awfullest heartbreakingest thing you ever saw."

"Oh, God."

"Well, years ago they had a daughter." He took Linnie by the arm and led her out of the bunk room, toward the stove where she'd spread the blankets on top of the rug. He set her down on it like a picnic blanket in a grease-stained concrete meadow. "And Foster—it was his brother-in-law who owned this place. Name was Calhoun."

"Spooky name."

"I know it. His first name was Smiley and they . . . you want a pillow?"

"A pillow?"

"I think those pillows in there were okay." Linnie watched him. Inside the bunk room he took a pillow out from beside Tommie and put his hand over where her head was. "It's okay," he whispered. "I'm sorry. We're okay. I'll come back in to you as soon as I can."

He came out with the pillow. "They were as close as close can be. It was Smiley who introduced Foster to his sister.

"He was best man at their wedding. He never married because he was . . . a little off. Not dumb—he was just one foot in his own world. Always half a smile, a wandering eye."

"Hence the name."

"Exactly. Foster, he was as sound a man as there is. And stern where Smiley was off-kilter. But the two of them, they cowboyed all over this place together in the fifties and sixties. They'd go out before daybreak, just the two of them, razors and combs in their pockets, jerk and crackers and baling wire in their bags and off they went for five, eight, ten days at a stretch. Sometimes working, sometimes just crisscrossing the tableland and nosing through the trees on horseback. Calhoun never married, so Foster's wife—the sick lady—she was mom for everyone. She was something of a drinker. But nice. They were a kind of a weird family up here, helped each other out over the years. Anyway, two, three years into the marriage Foster and Calhoun's sister finally have a baby girl."

"What's her name?"

"Emily."

"You and your Emilys."

"Linnie, it's the same girl."

She raised an eyebrow. "I don't get it."

"You stay out here two nights with me and see for yourself."

"She's a ghost?"

"Listen to the story."

"I thought you snatched her from some swing set."

"Hey," he said. "I'm figuring this out as I go. Do you want to know the rest?"

"Go, go."

"She's a nice enough kid. Emily Rose. Soft swoop of pale hair and little stony blue eyes. Not particularly pretty, or smart, just a girl, right?"

Linnie shook her head. "You are such a sexist."

"Oh, spare me, Linnie. She was just a dumb girl, okay? There are dumb boys too."

"Go on."

"Anyway, this kid turns ten or eleven, and around this time Calhoun decides he wants a shop. This shop. So of course he calls on Foster to help. They put the place up themselves—they're hard workers and decent guys, good builders, they pay attention to the craft, right? First thing they do is they dig the foundation. They rent a backhoe and they make it a big project. An early summer project. They pour the footers, they tie the rebar, they pour the cement pad and place the bolts to secure the steel poles. They bolt the wall frames and use this truss-type design"—he looks at Linnie and points up again—"to erect the roof. All of this takes well over a month—much longer than it needed to. For the first ten days, everything goes fine. Every day the wife comes down to the cabin with the kid and they make big suppers. Fried chicken and early salad and potatoes and lemonade. Pork chops and macaroni salad. Then Foster helps his wife clean up and Calhoun piddles around outside while the kid scrambles over the rock and up into the old cotton-woods. This is how it goes, right? They're digging the foundation and pouring the concrete and pil-ing dirt here and the backhoe's scooping earth from this side of the fence and dumping it on that side of the fence and they bring in a roll of corrugated steel, right?"

Linnie adjusted the pillow and looked up at him.

"All the while this kid is running dumb all over the place—up this pile of dirt and pounding on the sheet metal like a wild goat and up in the tree and hands in the concrete and then all of a sudden at lunch one day—she's supposed to be bringing in the sun tea—they can't find her. Just disappeared. They don't know where or how, but of course the wife tells the sheriff and the sheriff's posse comes out on horseback and for two weeks they run a comb of men and horses over this whole pasture and up into the skirt of the mountain looking for any sign of this kid. Dark birds of prey swinging against the hyperblue sky, men in their sweat-stained hats disappearing into the shimmering heat, into the tall columns of white trees.Week three they bring out the cadaver dogs and of course they don't find anything. In their grief and in their frenzy Calhoun and Foster finish the shop. Very carefully, very deliberately, to keep them sane, right? They keep it empty and cold as a tomb all that first winter, but eventually—because the thing is so useful—Calhoun starts using it. Practically moves in. Lets the cabin go."

"That's why it's such a wreck?"

"Exactly. And I'll tell you something, Linnie. You feel watched in this place."

"Really?"

"So many people have attested to seeing this girl that the first guy who was going to buy it—he'd put in a bid and everything—he found out after the offer was approved that the place is haunted and—get this—he legally got out of the bind."

"No shit."

"So."

"And this kid is still haunting the place?"

"Not only. Foster comes down here every god-damned night with a flashlight."

"You're shitting me."

"I'm serious, Linnie. We can wait for him tonight."

"Just looking for her?"

"Whatever happened to her, I say either Calhoun or Foster knew. Kept it under his hat all the rest of his days."

"Can you imagine keeping that kind of thing from your own wife? Or sister?"

"Foster's a miserable old man, Linnie."

"And he's just tortured by it."

"My thought is whatever happened, happened fast. And that old Smiley—let's say it was Calhoun who did it. Or maybe he didn't even kill her. He was just there when she fell—something like that, right? But he was implicated by his own guilt—who knows why, who knows what the guy's story was. He was quicker or crazier than people gave him credit for."

"And you've seen this kid?" She grins. "This ghost?"

"Linnie." He bent over her in the dark, put his mouth to her ear. "I've *talked* to her."

"Uh-huh. Come here. My hands are like ice. What does she say?"

"She's in love with me."

"Of course she is."

"No, seriously. She wants to live with me forever. She wants me to marry her. She wants to bear me ghost babies. Here. Lift."

"I don't know if I like the way this is going."

"This or the story?"

"The story."

"The floor's not too hard."

"No."

"Turn around. Here, take the pillow."

"Will you tell me another story?"

"I'll just tell you the next chapter. I'll tell you what happened when I went into that bunk room and found her little dead self tucked in with the mice running all over her face."

"God! David that's awful. I'm trying to kiss you here. Can it wait?"

"It's a better story in the dark, anyway."

Linnie looked up at our guy and grinned. "Oh, shut up."

. . . . .

Tommie stood for a long time in her nightgown facing the closed door to the shop and breathing, listening, holding her breath, listening: nothing. Wood hissing and snapping in the hot stove. Eight o'clock and dark as midnight. Their voices would have stopped humming some time ago. But she'd know they hadn't gone inside, or washed the dishes.

She held her breath tight in her little freckled chest when she opened the door, just three inches and without a sound, and remained still and looking into the shop as her eyes adjusted to the light. Moonlight drenched the concrete floor and the pile of blankets where the two adults lay moving together before the stove. The white shape of Lamb's face looked up at her, over the crown of Linnie's head. So much light in the room Tommie could see where it made a white shining stripe in Linnie's dark hair. Lamb's eyes were blue-white in the silver dark. His face was at first twisted up in concentration but then it fell open, his eyes fell open, and a little smile. Tommie didn't back away. She didn't catch her breath or cry. She stood watching. Ten seconds, twenty seconds, thirty seconds. He loved her for it. Her mouth a little open, her eyes open, stunned, transfixed. Lamb paused only a moment and Linnie lifted her head, reached up, and put her hands on the sides of his face so he moved again, smiling down at Linnie and lifting his face toward

Tommie, their eyes deadlocked. He remained silent as he moved, watching Tommie, and when he finally shut his eyes and lifted his chin, teeth clenched, Tommie closed the door and stepped back into her room and crawled into the sleeping bag where she fell asleep, face pasted to the vinyl with tears and snot until Lamb came in and very gently, very carefully, woke her saying now, my dear, you know all my secrets. You are practically living inside of my heart.

"You're wearing your nightgown."

She nodded.

"You still love me, don't you?"

"Yes," she whispered.

"Do you have to go the bathroom? Come. Come outside." He opened the side door of the bunk room that opened to the old horse tank. "Go ahead. Pull up your nightgown."

She hesitated. Looked at him and down at the dead grass and back up.

"Come on," he said. "You're going back in that room in twenty minutes. We don't have all night."

When she finished he put his jacket over her and they hiked out a small distance from the shop and sat on the cold grass beside the dark rivulets of water running off the river and into the beds of brown pigweed and dead goldenrod.

"What do I call you now? David?"

Lamb kept his head down. His eyes filled. "Come here," he said. He took her between his legs, her back against his chest. "It's like you're Emily." He brushed her hair back off her face and tucked it into the hood of his jacket.

"That was a game."

"No it wasn't," he said quickly. He turned her face to him. "Take it back. It's not a game. Everything I do in my life from here on out is to protect us, to protect this thing we've discovered. Do you understand? You're braver than I am, Tom. I haven't always had nice people in my life. It makes me behave a little erratically sometimes, right? I didn't exactly know what was going on when we met. I didn't know where this was headed. Do you believe me?"

Nod.

"It doesn't matter what we call each other, does it? That's just names."

"I don't know."

"Whatever you call me—John, or retard, or son of a bitch . . ." She smiled at this. ". . . you would still know my true heart, wouldn't you? You know me, don't you?"

"Yes."

"I know you do. It's extraordinary. Come here. Closer. Yes. It's cold, isn't it? No one's ever known me as you do. You smell like a healthy little animal." His face was very serious now. "We've seen each other, haven't we, Tom. Do you understand that this doesn't happen with other people? I don't know what to say about it. I know what other people might say." He pressed his thumb hard into the little plate of bones where her ribs gathered just beneath her breasts. She blinked and watched him. "The body doesn't lie, Tom. It doesn't know how."

"Are you and that lady?"

"It wasn't what you're thinking. I will tell you what it was—I'll tell you every detail. But when the situation is reversed, Tom"—his eyes filled and his voice cracked—"I don't want to know, okay?" He was whispering now, fat tears coming down his old wrinkled face. "Don't tell me, okay? Swear you won't tell me."

"Does she still like you?"

"She's in love with me, yes."

"Do you like her?"

"Look at me, Tom. Look me right in the eye. No. I don't like her even a little bit. I sort of hate her, even. And I don't use that word lightly. She's spoiled and selfish."

"Sounds like Sidney."

"That's a good way to think of her. Like a grown-up Sidney."

"Does she want to marry you?"

"I think she might. Is this okay? Can I hold you like that?"

Nod. "How long is she staying?"

"One more day. Maybe two. I'm going to stay with her for us, do you understand?"

"I should stay in the bunk room."

"You should?"

"I should stay there until she leaves. She won't even know I'm here."

"You're sure?"

"What else will we do?"

"No," he said. "You're right. You're sort of a step ahead of me." He grinned at her.

She ran her palm up against her nose and sniffled. "It's no big deal," she said. "It'll be like camping."

"In the bunk room?"

"Yes."

"And I'll come visit you when it's safe, right?"

"Okay."

"And you can go out this side door to pee. Right?"

"Okay."

"And when you know we're out in the cabin— you'll know because I'll leave that little desk light on as a signal. You know the desk light on the work-bench? I'll leave it on when it's safe for you to come out and raid the fridge, by which I mean the cooler, right?"

"Okay."

He lifted her chin and kissed her mouth. "You'll still call me Gary, won't you? Promise me you will. Promise me you always always will."

"Why?"

"Because no one else in the world calls me Gary. You're the only one who knows me this way. Like I'm the only one who knows you as Emily. They're our true names. If you could see through my flesh"—he took her hand and put it on his chest—"Gary would be the name written across my heart." He kissed her on the temple and the forehead and the mouth. "You were wonderful." He kissed. "You saved us, do you know that? Just like you said you would. And we have luck on our side. I want to tell you something, okay? Something I've never told anyone in my life."

"What?" She sat up a little and looked at him.

"I'm telling you this so you'll understand how precious you are to me. It's about my brother."

"You have a brother?"

"Three brothers."

"Oh."

"You won't tell anybody about this, will you, Tom? You'll give me your word?"

She nodded.

"My littlest brother, Tommie. He disappeared."

"Where?"

"Nobody knows. He was just your age, just a little bit older. He was twelve."

"He was kidnapped?"

Lamb was whispering now. "I don't know, we never knew. He used to sleep behind the gas station, in his sleeping bag."

"Why?"

"Our house was kind of a sad place. I think you know how that can be. And one morning he just . . . didn't show up. Didn't come back."

"Not ever?"

"Not ever."

She was quiet a moment.

And look. The two days that Lamb and Linnie and Tom spent arranged in this way—the dark early mornings with Tommie in the bunk room, she in her beautiful nightgown and he in his big sheepskin coat; breakfast with Linnie back in the cabin, back in the fold-out couch—the AM radio and eating canned sausages and mandarin oranges with their fingers; the evenings of sitting with Linnie beside the fire in the cold, sharing a cigarette in the dark, the smell of snow and cold dirt and dead grass in the wind; running a piece of chocolate or a kiss or a surprising mouthful of whiskey to the girl in her snug little sleeping bag nest. So much love

all over everyone—they were sweet days for everybody. Any one of them would tell you so.

. . . . .

It was late afternoon and already dark when Linnie
and Lamb woke on the fold-out couch under piles
of blankets and the heavy throw rug he'd pulled
over the top of all of it. She sat up and looked out
the window behind them.

"Hey," Lamb said, "why don't you lie still and let
a man sleep."

"There's someone out there on your road. Actually, two someones."

David sat up beside her and they watched a white
suburban follow a black jeep.

"They're going to Foster's."

"The old man?"

"His wife is dying down there."

"Oh. How sad."

"She's all hooked up to machines and in the same
bed all the time. I've seen him wash her face with a
bowl of soapy water and a washcloth."

"So sad."

"Sometimes the caretaker goes first. Know what
that means?"

"What?"

"I'm going to have to find some backup girls to assist me on my deathbed."

"Oh, please, you act like you're an old man."

"I am an old man."

"You are not."

Lamb got up and poured some of the steel-cold river water outside the door into the enamel coffeepot and set it on the woodstove. He opened the door and turned the wood, added another piece.

"Do you think they need help with something? Seems like a lot of activity, doesn't it?" She was up on her knees looking out at the road, the blankets pulled up around her shoulders.

"What I think," he said, and tore off the rug and the blankets one at a time to reveal her, bare and shivering on the dusty threadbare couch, "is that there's a cold front moving in."

"Yeah, you think?" She reached across the couch for one of the blankets in his hand.

"We'll get the first big snow. It's time," he said and appraised the sky. "Maybe they're just stocking up down there, having the visiting nurse come in and straighten up camp and make sure everything's in working order before the snow falls."

Clouds drooped and condensed and there was a wet white circle of vapor around the sun.

"Think we'll get snowed in?"

"Maybe, if it drifts. It's covered up the windows before."

"Snow cave."

"We'll gather up all the blankets on the property and load them up on our bed, and board up the bathroom window, right?"

"Okay."

"I have a lot of stock in the shop. We'll bring in piles of it so we don't have to move from the stove here."

Lamb and Linnie watched the front come in, the clouds sagging and seeming to fall between them and on top of the cabin and shop. While they ate their canned stew and pan-fried biscuits in the cabin, the wind finally stopped. The tree outside the window went completely still. The constant rush and clatter of the wind went dead, and the snow came. It came light and gently and fell straight down like gauzy curtains and it was thick and heavy and wet— odd snow for fall in the mountains. A low groan rumbled around them. Thunder and snow. Lamb shook his head and held Linnie on the pull-out couch before the window.

"It's wonderful. It looks like the lightning is going to touch the ground."

"Because we're so high up."

"Can't I come live with you and be your love?"

"You'd get tired of it out here. There's nothing to do."

"You'd be here."

"Oh, you. Come here."

The night was mild, the snow poured like still pools of white milk into the ditches and over the dirt road and in every crack and crevice until everything was blue-white in the dark. Lamb did not leave Linnie's side all night, trusting his girl to sleep tight and warm in the shop. In the small hours the wind picked up again and swept all the snow clouds south and east and what snow had fallen piled up in drifts against the shop and cabin and across the road.

It was only just past dark, very early in the morning, when they were both awakened by a knock at the door. Lamb pulled on his Levi's and peeked out and opened the door. A fine smoke of snow blew in at foot level. When he opened the door the man spoke in a low voice, and it was for Lamb as though his head was filling up with snow, his thinking brain temporarily blanked out, eclipsed by the sudden flash of danger.

"She had the fire built up good in the shed and swore she was all right," the man said, indicating Tommie, "but she looked a little bugged out to me."

Tommie glanced up at Lamb, her face very still and her lips white. "My stomach hurts," she said.

Lamb stumbled as he opened the door wider, looking back into the room at Linnie, who was wrapped in the blanket and the rug. She sat up straight but could not move. She was not wearing any clothes. Unthinking, he opened his arms to the girl and she went to him, teary and dead silent.

"Stomachache like you'll throw up?"

She shook her head in his flannel shirt.

"Dad said you had a snowplow we might use. Didn't think you'd be awake, thought I'd return it later this morning."

"Oh," Lamb said, smiling and looking stupidly from the man to Linnie, ignoring the girl now. "Oh good. Yes, sure."

"Is she okay?" the man asked Lamb, and suddenly Linnie saw that, somehow, this child was Lamb's and did not belong to the man at the door. She was the ghost, the dead girl, the girl swept off the swing set. Linnie's mouth went sour and her limbs went hot and liquid and when she spoke she heard her voice as if it were coming from someone else, someone outside of her.

"Who is that, David?"

He made a sheepish face. "Linnie, this is my niece."

"Emily?"

Lamb gave Linnie an odd smile. "That's right."

Lamb raised his index finger at Linnie to shush her and turned to the man at the door. Linnie stood, the blankets and rug wrapped around her, and immediately sat down again. She looked at the child not with sympathy or concern but with rage. The girl did not look at Linnie.

"It's a not a shed," the girl said. "There's a whole bedroom."

Linnie stared at her.

"That's right," Lamb said. "Bunk beds and books and blankets and snacks." He looked down at the child and smiled at her, then winked at the man in the doorway.

"Everything's okay here, then?" the man asked again.

"Sure, we're great," David said, and he wrapped Tommie in an afghan and sat her on the edge of the pull-out couch beside Linnie. The two did not look at each other. Tommie's eyes were fixed to the cabin floor and Linnie's upon Lamb.

"What about you? Are you down at the Fosters'?"

The man outside the door finally extended his hand. "I'm Emory Foster. My mother passed away day before yesterday."

"Oh." David shifted his eyes and his weight. "I'm sorry to hear that. It must hurt." He ignored Linnie and Tommie completely now, kept his eyes and attention entirely upon the man. "How is your father doing? Can we help?"

"Well, actually he asked me if I'd come down here and just let you know. My wife's up there with him now, and we'll be expecting Doug Michaels—the county coroner—an old family friend. He'll be along shortly."

"Okay."

"We just got a couple drifts in the drive and"—he looked out behind him at the road—"I think most of this will clear up through the day, but I can plow us a straight line from here to the house while I'm at it."

"Please. Go right ahead. Or"—he touched his chest—"do you want me to do it? Maybe you want to be inside with your father and wife?"

"Oh, no. Little air will do me good. I'd appreciate it. I'll bring back a second cleared line when I return the plow. Make it easier on Doug that way."

"Well." Lamb looked for the first time at Linnie and Tommie, then back to Emory. "Fact is we were all planning on shipping out today."

Tommie and Lamb glanced at each other.

"We were just going to make a family breakfast the three of us and ship out."

Emory nodded. "Okay. Well, I'll do this right away and get back case you need it too." He looked back again, at the girl, and at Linnie. "Though I think it'll clear up pretty quick."

"It's a bright sun at this altitude."

"It is."

"Emory." Lamb extended his hand again. "I'm so sorry."

"Thanks." He leaned into the house and waved. "Good to meet you, Emily. Hope you're feeling better soon."

She looked at the man in the doorway but said nothing.

Emory Foster pushed the snowplow from the drive up the road into the jewelry of early winter. Lamb stooped down and asked the child if she wanted hot chocolate, then asked if the fire was still going in the shed. Linnie sat frozen in place while Lamb put on his boots to walk Tommie outside. As he was stepping out into the snow, he turned back.

"You want some hot chocolate too, Linnie?"

"Sure. No. David?"

"I'll be right back. It's a bit of an odd situation but everybody's okay, I'll tell you in a minute. I just want to see about her stomach and make sure she doesn't have a fever. She's been sick. I didn't want you getting sick."

"You didn't even say."

"It's okay. Everybody's okay. I'll be right back." And he pulled the door shut and went back out into the shop with Tommie.

And they hadn't a minute alone again—not David and Linnie nor Linnie and the girl. David explained he really should take the girl back to her mother, her fever had broken but she wasn't well and the time they were going to spend out here fishing and camping had pretty much been snowed out. Her father—my little brother Nel, he explained—died years ago and it had fallen to Lamb to be the occasional father figure.

"She never remarried?"

"She tried once—twice, actually—but it was no good."

"Sad."

"It is. You would've liked Nel."

"How much younger was he?"

"Four years."

"Oh."

"He was a blondie."

"I'm sorry, David. I didn't know."

"Let's reschedule this for . . . first of the year, you and me. We'll rent something with big wheels and come back out, right? Drive through the nineteen feet of snow."

"I'd love that."

"This seems like a bad time doesn't it. Emily sick, Foster's wife suddenly gone, unexpected snow. Let's all get home. I'll take the girl back to her mother."

"It's Chicago?"

"Michigan. Muskegon."

"Ah."

"Her mother drove her to Chicago, but I'll take her all the way back up."

Linnie nodded.

"David."

"Lin."

"Why the story? About the kid who disappeared?"

He lifted his chin, a thin-lipped smile on his face, as if to convince the day around him that he was smiling and not about to sob again like a boy. There'd been enough of that.

"Now that we can be . . . you know . . . closer, you'll learn more about my family."

"And you mine," she said. "But I don't understand."

"Be patient with me, Lin. Please. I need that from you."

She was quiet a moment and studied him. He smiled.

"Excuse me just a minute, will you?"

Lamb went to the girl in the shop to help her gather up her own things while Linnie packed up her car.

. . .

"We get the afternoon together," he told Tommie.

"We do?"

"And the night. And tomorrow. And the next day. Our last day."

"Three days?"

"We'll have you home on day twenty. That's almost four times as long as we originally said."

"I know."

"Do you forgive me?"

"I wanted to stay."

"It wasn't my idea?"

"It was our idea."

"Equal partners?"

"Equal partners."

"Good. Sweetheart, listen. She'll be gone within the hour. You stay put and I'll get dressed."

When Lamb was loading up Linnie's rental, checking the air pressure in the tires and the oil for her, his shirt sleeves rolled up to his elbows, she went into the shop, rooted around in the cooler for a snack for the road, put a Little Debbie cake and a can of pineapple juice into her purse, walked over to the bunk room door, stood before it. Just a moment. Then she walked over to the woodstove and rubbed her hands before rejoining Lamb on the driveway, where she wrapped her arms around his waist from behind and kissed his neck.

"Let's move out here to live."

"How about we try a single week in the middle of winter and see how much you still like it?" He turned around to face her.

"I can't wait to see you in Chicago."

"You tell Wilson I'm doing good by you."

"You think he knows?"

"You're just a dumb kid sometimes." He grinned, and they loaded her up. "The whole reason I invited you out here was so I'd be able to keep my job." She started the engine and rolled down the window.

"I'll call you from the airport and leave you messages."

"I love your messages."

"I might have to whisper them, so turn up the volume on your phone."

He turned a dial near the side of his head. "All my ears are on."

"Mine too."

"Kiss me."

"See you in six days."

"Six days. Put your seat belt on."

• • • • •

The girl was savage inside the bunk room.

"And she'll tell, and you'll go to jail, and every-one will know, and I'll get in so much trouble."

"Listen, listen. Tommie. Please."

"You didn't keep us secret."

"Tommie," he raised his voice. "Now I don't want to yell but you're not listening to me. I know Linnie better than you do, right? Please take your hands from your face."

"She's going to tell."

"Please take your hands from your face, Tommie, I can't understand you."

And she said something, and something, something, and took her hands from her face.

"Look, Tommie, if she thought anything she would have told me. She would have probably been very upset. But I just sent her back into the world with plans to see her the day after I drop you at your mother's."

"You did?"

"I did. She went off smiling to the airport. She loves me."

"Oh."

"Do you believe me?"

"If you don't like her, why are you going to see her?"

"For us, Tom. For you and me. To keep us safe."

"Oh."

"Sometimes you just know a person, Tom. Linnie isn't strong like us. She doesn't always see the kinds of things we see. Do you understand? You want a little taste of whiskey from my mouth? Here. Come on. Let me scoop you up and carry you to the couch. We'll hang out and catch up. You can tell me all the dreams you had while I was busy."

"Okay."

"This is the beginning of the part where we take you back home," he said, kicking the shop door open with his boot and carrying the girl outside and into the cabin. "In light of all the promises we made to keep each other safe. The part where we take you back to Lombard and your mother who loves you, and I'll come back here, and if Linnie ever says anything, or realizes she saw you, there'll be no girl out here, right? No one for anybody to find. And you'll be home safe." He laid her down on the couch and put a pillow beneath her head.

"But they'll ask me where I was."

Lamb gave the girl a look of alarm. "But you won't tell them?"

She shook her head.

He made like he was wiping sweat from his forehead. "I thought for a minute you'd just been setting me up this whole time."

They set up a dinner camp on the river and the
girl opened two cans of sliced potatoes and a can of
corned beef hash. It hissed and snapped in the hot
metal pan, and Lamb watched the girl turn it until
all the pan was greased.

"Watch the heat," he said.

"I am."

"Not too high."

"I know."

"Here. Move it here."

"I can do it."

They sat hip to hip in the dirt, the scrappy river
trees hunching over them.

"You're turning into a fine little camping
woman."

"Thanks."

"Ready for eggs?" He handed them to her, one at
a time. "Don't break those yolks."

"I won't."

He sat very still to record the moment in his
blood, to fill up his lungs, drink up the cold air and
the smell of water and melting snow. Beside him
the lines of her hands and skinny arms moving skill-
fully in the twilight.

"Those are our last eggs."

"I know."

"Next time," he said, "it'll be potatoes, fried eggs, and fresh trout."

"When will that be?"

"Your eighteenth birthday."

"Deal."

"But maybe you won't want to leave your life to come and see me. I'll be really, really old. What if I'm dying in a small, stale hospital room all alone?"

"I'll sneak you out."

They ate with forks, huffing the eggs and hash around in their mouths and lifting their chins and laughing at each other. Balancing the hash and a bit of yellow-soaked egg in each bite. Competing between them for the perfect forkful. By the time they'd finished their hands were sticky and the mess kits gritty with dirt and blackened by fire. The girl had her legs and feet tucked beneath her in the grass. He patted her little belly.

"All those boys are going to be crowding you when you get back and they see how you've changed." He put the tin plates and cups inside the metal pan and fitted all the mess kit together and tightened the red canvas strap. The sky was luminous behind his head. "I don't think I could stand seeing you in Chicago again, Tom. You'll lose interest in your old friend and I couldn't bear that. I don't think I could stand even being in the same city as you. If you know what I mean."

Tommie lay back and looked up at cold white stars caught up in the tree branches, corn-colored leaves caught up in her hair, her white teeth blue in the new dark, while he set everything in his pack and carried river water in his hands to the fire to put it out. When they were back at the cabin he took a pen and piece of paper from the glove compartment of the truck and leaned over the hood. She watched him write. "Forget I'm doing this, okay?" Then he walked her, holding her hand, down among the rotted fence posts. "Watch your feet. We'll just be a minute." He took her hand and put it on the jagged splintered top of a fence post as if she were blind. "Feel that? Memorize that. It's the fourteenth one from the house. Fourteenth fence post on the fourteenth day. Can you remember that?"

"Why?"

"I'm going to leave this fence post up, right? No matter how rotted it gets. No matter how much home improvement happens around it. The fourteenth fencepost will always stand here for you." He drove the tiny folded piece of paper deep into the split wood of the post. "Turn around," he said. "Turn around and look at our little house. And the waving grass, and the silver moon. You see? It's ours, right?" He put his finger beneath her chin and turned her head up to his. "I will it to you, Tommie. It's yours. It is maybe more yours than it was ever mine. You'll come back here after I'm gone, won't you? And move right in. I'll have written you letters. I'll write you half a dozen letters every day for the rest of my life, and I'll hide them everywhere. In the mugs and in old socks. You'll have to go through everything and piece them all together in a line. You can hang each one with a clothespin out in the sun and they'll tell the story of my love for you. If you have a husband, you'll have to leave him behind until you've sorted through it all, right? All these messages from me. Messages from the dead."

"I don't want to go back."

"Ssh. Feel that?" He pressed his thumb between her breasts. "That pressure right there? That's the world calling you." He picked her up like a child, up on his hip, and carried her to the bottom bunk. She breathed into the cloth of his shirt. He knew she was picturing his love notes out on a clothesline in the bright wind. He knew she was picturing him dead.

• • • • •

It's the kind of thing a guy like David Lamb might tell himself again and again, how she'd lifted her head, the little crinkles and puckers in her chin and neck as she looked down at him and that absolutely terrified and wide-open face, white in the dark, and shadows from the oil lamp shrinking and stretching like live arms. And him telling her God, God, you're sweet, you have freckles everywhere. And how he'd choked up telling her he was so honored to see so many of them, and were they his? Could they say they were his? Such an expensive gift. So dear. And listen to me: he knew it.

Watching her load up the truck the next morning in her miniature parka, he saw her in her purple tube top, pushed around by those stupid girls. All her body and inner world had come awake by his hand. Her cheeks and the tip of her nose were bright pink in the cold. She sniffled and ran her sleeve above her lip.

"Emily Tom. Before we go. Will you lie with me in the deer beds by the water?"

"Okay."

"Can I ask you something?"

"What."

"Will you . . ." He looked down at his hands, and into her face, and down again. "Will you wear your nightgown?"

She looked at her blue jeans and jacket. "You'll have to keep me warm."

"I will."

Eventually our old guy would look to her like a fluke, a mistake, a weird time she survived when she was eleven. In his memory she would become more beautiful, more dear. In hers, he'd be a monster.

· · · · ·

All of eastern Wyoming and western Nebraska were hammered by ice and driving wind. The girl shivered in the passenger seat, her lips white, with Lamb sweating beside her, a giant bright orange bottle of cough medicine between them and Styrofoam cups of hot tea from gas stations. Every half hour or so Lamb reached sideways to touch her face and she'd open her eyes and try to smile.

"You look awful," she'd say.

"You look worse."

In Grand Island he reached into the back and retrieved the filthy Cubs hat and put it on her head. They stopped for egg drop soup in Omaha and slept twelve hours in a Holiday Inn with the TV on where they were sick and feverish and both their bodies aching. Back in the truck he fed her Nyquil and ginger ale and she slept or spoke brokenly and deliriously until Council Bluffs. By the time they made Des Moines they were both coming out of the fog of medicine and sore throats and splitting temples. Lamb drove them back to the little green motel now bleak with dark wet leaves.

"Did you like me when we stayed here the first time? I think you did."

"I think I did," she said.

"How did you know?"

"Just knew."

"Do you still, Tom?"

"Yes."

"Even though I'm a liar and a thief?"

She reached out and punched him forcelessly in the shoulder.

"Boy," he said, "you were a lot stronger on the way out. We need to get you some spinach."

She grinned.

"Your body has changed since September," he said. "That part is true."

"I know."

He whispered. "Did I change it?"

She whispered back. "I think it was going to happen anyway."

His eyes filled with tears, the world went all smeary on the other side of the windshield. "You know just what to say." And suddenly he began sobbing. Really crying, really huffing tears. His whole chest seizing and his face twisted like a little boy's. What would be left him when she was gone: a hole that she'd once filled with these consoling words. His doubt and his demons, the ones he'd taught her to keep at bay, they'd get him by the throat. And he knew it.

"Promise me something, dear," he said. Say she'd gotten used to these bursts of crying—say he'd had a few of them. Say even that he'd been having them for a while, in the afternoons and a little bit in the mornings by the fire. "If you discover one day that you hate me."

"I won't."

"Please don't say that. You might. I have to say this, okay."

She waited. His voice was scratchy and high.

"If you discover you hate me, that you're angry with me, that I've ruined your life. When I'm ninety. Anytime." He stopped. She nodded for him to go on. She'd become such a little woman. "You'll come tell me, won't you? You'll buy a pair of steel-toed boots and come and find me all alone and dried up and sick in a nursing home and kick my fucking teeth in. Or whisper to me on my deathbed that I was d—"

"Stop it!" Now she was crying.

"Oh," he said and wiped his nose with his sleeve then hers and turned her crying face to his. "It's not true," he said. "I'm sorry. Nothing I said was true. I've had too much medicine. Too much driving." He took her hands and held them to his chest, to his neck, then his mouth. "Please forget everything I just said. Please promise me you will forget it. Tell me you promise, okay?"

"I promise."

It was the fever that'd cracked him open. Lamb had wanted to return her to her mother shipshape, twelve on a ten scale. The plan had been to bring her home fast, three days on the road and no time for this kind of slippage, but there it was. Everything was off. He felt ash filling up his chest and throat from the inside, blocking his mouth and thickening his heart and filling up his head, he hoped, blocking it out like the heavy gray ceiling of winter settling in over the plains, so that he would not be able to see into it. Not after this day. Not after this.

By the time they made Rockford he could see they needed to hold out there a day, maybe two days. Until she got well, until he was ready. He pulled into the registration parking space at a Red Roof off of I-90, just across the street from a shopping outlet. He held the steering wheel with both hands and stared hard through the windshield. "Do you want to know what it is? It's that I can't let you go." The girl did not speak. "Does that make you sorry? Like some part of you is anxious to get home?"

"I don't know." Her voice was very small.

"You sound scared. Are you scared?"

"No."

"Because you trust me, don't you?"

"Yes."

"Do you know what's going to happen to me when you're back in your life, swimming and going to movies and dances? Getting your first job and falling in love and cutting your hair short?"

"I don't know."

"You'll do all those things. It's okay. Tell me you will. Say it."

"I don't know, Gary."

"You will. You'll throw your tree book in the back of the closet and find it when you're packing for college. You'll throw it away. You should let me take that poisonous flower now. I'm the one who's going to need it."

"I won't throw the book away."

"Do you know how it will be for me?"

The girl said nothing.

"I'm going back to that shop and I'm going to sleep on the floor next to our bunk beds. I'm never going to sleep in them again. But I'm going to leave them up. I'll be on the wool blanket on the concrete. Every night, all winter, if it kills me."

"You'll freeze."

"It'll be good for me to feel that cold."

"Gary."

"When it's winter here and the wind bites your face and turns your fingers to glass inside your gloves, I want you to think of me alone out there."

"Gary, don't."

"No. Don't. Don't touch me. It's good for me to cry a little. A man can cry, can't he?"

She watched him holding the steering wheel.

"You'll outgrow me," he said. "You'll forget everything."

"No I won't."

"I'm going to write it all down. Send it to you. Or no. You'd better just forget all about me. I'll come back to the city and wander around looking for you, but you'll be gone. There'll be a woman in your place and I won't know how to find you."

"I can't help it."

"I know." He was really crying.

A businesswoman in a long beige raincoat and purple scarf passed before them and looked into the Ford. She opened the driver's side door of a blue Chrysler beside the girl, and Lamb wiped his eyes with his shirtsleeve.

"Look at this old guy," he said, "blubbering like a baby."

"You'll be okay, Gary."

"Oh, you dear thing."

"I think we should take a nap," the girl said, "in here."

"In the truck?"

"In this motel."

"You don't feel well, do you?"

"I'm okay."

"We're going to stay here as long as we need to, okay? I'm bringing you back healthy. I'm delivering you to your mother hale and whole, right? Our story depends on it."

"Right."

In the cool and damp motel room Lamb folded down the bed for the girl and arranged all the pillows while she showered, and when she came out shivering in the tiny white towel he scooped her up, naked and damp towel and all, and set her in the sheets and pulled the blankets over her.

"Now," he said and handed her the TV remote, "I'm going to be right back."

"Where are you going?"

"I'm going to get us more nighttime meds and hot soup from the Jewel over there and we'll just find an old movie or make fun of the news guys till we fill our bellies and fall asleep, right?"

"Okay."

"Good. What kind of soup?"

"The hot kind."

"Like spicy?"

"No, please."

"You want something with noodles in it, don't you?"

"Yes."

"Noodles and cold medicine and pillows and TV and sleep. Who doesn't want that? And tomorrow, fried eggs and hot coffee."

"Gary?"

"Yes, my dear."

"I don't actually feel sick anymore."

"We just want to give you a little more soup and medicine and sleep so you're really strong. Okay?"

"Okay."

"We don't want you having a relapse."

"Okay."

"Tom?"

"Yes."

"When I get back"—he pointed to the bed—"can I lay there? In the space beside you?"

"Duh."

"I didn't want to make any assumptions."

She rolled her eyes and grinned. "I'll find something on TV."

"Be right back, my dear."

· · · · ·

Imagine you're in bed. That little old twin bed, back at home. The sheets wrinkled and soft and cool. Your legs clean and strong. Your shoulders sliding down your back, just melting away. Right?

Say you're reading a book. You let it fall a little, into your knees or upon the satin edging of a deep vanilla-colored plush. Cars shushing past outside. You're just napping in there, just resting and reading, your body recharging. You can barely read the print on the page. The truth is you'll feel a cold and empty sagging at the bottom of your heart. Everything outside is metal. Your body will feel a little blank. It wants my warm arms and legs beside it, right? It wants our old open sky outside our little bunk room windows. It wants the river and the soft purring of the nightjars perched in the trees, and it wants the wild grass seeds in your hair and in your little white socks. It wants the heat of our little breakfast fire in the mornings, how it warms your chest and the fronts of your arms and shoulders and opens all the pores in your face and repeats itself in your eyes. Fresh breeze cooling your back. The smell of sage and the smell of snow on the wind. Hands wrapped around your little metal cup of instant. You'll be in your little gray city room, lost to me. A thousand miles away. The little bunks and the barbed wire and the withering bluebonnets gone. And you'll turn into your pillow and wonder was I ever real? Was it all a dream?

There will be such an awful beauty in your heart. A wound like a seal upon it. It will lie over all the cracked and hard city like a soft, bright-colored

film. Your own face overlaid with the face you
wore when you were with me in the mountains. A
brighter face, a younger face, a soft one that mirrors
the weather. You'll read books—little paperbacks—
looking for the kind of sentence that keeps the
wound alive. And you must keep it alive. Don't you
ever forget this hurt. Don't you ever forget what
you've seen with me. It will save you. You'll be like
an apple tree among all the ash-colored buildings of
that granite city. Close your eyes. Turn away from
the book in your lap, turn away from the sounds
of everyone around you. Take a slow deep breath.
Listen. It's the sound of the wind rushing through
the box elder outside our window. It's the sound of
me whispering. I'll be with you this way.

· · · · ·

The two left the motel in the morning, before the
sun was up. The frontage road was quiet, traffic
lights still blinking red, gas stations bright in the
bleary cold. Everything was over. The day was a
shade cooler, a shade grayer than the day before.

"Last day," he said when they pulled out of a
Chevron station. Little cold needles of rain turned
to sleet. "And here comes winter."

"It's only October."

"That's ice," he said, nodding at the windshield.

When they came into Lombard the streets were black with rain and ice, the parking lots of grocery stores and strip malls nearly empty.

"Nobody's up," Lamb said.

"Lucky for us."

"Desolate as the field behind the cabin," he said. "That stretch to the base of the mountains. See? You'll find that same openness if you look for it."

She cried deep and shaking and coughing sobs, and he pulled over in front of an empty pharmacy so she could get it out. Snot ran down the girl's face and he reached across to wipe the tears from her cheekbones and chin. He leaned in and caught them with his mouth, and kissed her with his eyes open, checking the parking lot around them.

"Right?" he whispered, and she nodded. "This is how we said it would go, didn't we?" She closed her eyes and opened them and closed them. "I never lied to you, did I?"

"No."

"Didn't I let you stay longer with me?" Then he straightened her yellow sweater, brushing it down with an open palm. She watched him. "I'll make you a promise, okay?" He leaned in and spoke with his face very close to hers. "Valentine's Day," he said. "I'll come find you, right? We can be together for a little while. That's less than four months."

"You will?"

"Just over a hundred days. Can you carry this that long?"

"You'll come back to get me?"

"I'll come visit. I'll be very careful, and I'll protect you. Right?"

She nodded.

"We'll go back to our white hotel. Or out to those little falls by the river. I'll send you a sign. And when you see it you'll wait there for me. And I'll take you away in this wonderful old truck for an hour, or two or three, right? You'll have to keep your eyes open all the time for the sign from me."

"What will it be?"

"A ribbon tied some unlikely place. Or at Christmastime, a tiny blue lightbulb in a string of white lights. Or a broken window, like that little broken window in the cabin."

She was crying all over again.

"Oh, sweetie," he said. "Oh, sweetie, it's your cabin. It will always be yours. I'm going to leave it for you. Didn't I say I would? And you can live there forever when I'm gone."

"Maybe." She was trying to say something.

"I can't understand you."

"Maybe in a few years?"

"Yes."

"Maybe we could just tell everyone."

"I think you may be right," he said and again wiped the tears from her face with the back of his sleeve. "I think it may have to be that way."

"I think. They. Would under. Stand." Her chest heaving up and down and her words froggy.

"Because it's love, isn't it?"

She nodded and ran the inside of her hand up against her wet nose.

He drove slowly out of the parking lot and onto the street. "You remember the plan, right?"

"Yes."

"Now, Tom. You have to collect yourself. You have to be brave. Remember all the things we said about keeping everyone safe."

"I know."

"Can you stop crying now?"

"I'm trying."

"This is how it has to be for a little while."

"I know."

"You keep yourself well and strong so when I come back for you everyone will believe it was good for you, right? Doesn't that make sense?"

"Yes."

"If I come back for you, and you've been a hysterical mess, everyone will say I'm no good for you, won't they?"

Nod.

"Good girl."

He drove out onto Butterfield Road, and there were the tall rectangles of the girl's triplet concrete apartment buildings off in the distance, less than a mile up the road, the ones they'd been picturing in all their conversations and dreams when they had been surrounded by trees and river and wind. Here they were, real and tall and solid and filled with sleeping people, the girl's mother up there, and Jessie, half the window squares bright yellow, lit up like an unfinished game in the gloom.

"Couldn't we? We go somewhere?" Her face ugly and red. "You could have. Coffee."

He shook his head. "I'm sorry, baby. This is the last chapter. We knew it was coming. We have to be strong. When you get to have a love like this you have to be strong enough to bear it. A love like ours is expensive. Think of it that way. And we pay for it with the next empty string of days. I know you're good for it. I've always known."

She nodded and looked down at the backpack between her feet.

"You know what to do if they've moved, right?"

"Yes."

"Tell me."

"I tell the security guard I ran away in September but here I am and would he help me find my mother."

"And you'll be strong and beautiful. Say it."

"I'll be strong and beautiful."

"And you won't cry when you say it. You'll be just perfectly self-possessed."

"Yes."

"You know I can't stop," he said when they were a block away.

"I know."

He pointed, then regripped her hand. "I'm going to slow down right up there. Twelve seconds and you hop out and take your backpack and go."

"Okay."

"Okay. Ready?" It took less than ten seconds.

"Wait."

"Here we are. I can't kiss you here."

She took the ball cap off her own head and pushed it toward him. "You should keep it."

"Ready set go. Good-bye, Tommie."

She opened the door and hopped out shaking in her fleece, impossibly bright in all the gray around her, and she dragged the backpack after her and it was over. She stood on the corner watching David Lamb steer back into his lane and through the yellow light. A moment later she started run-ning after him in her boots, dragging her backpack crookedly behind her, alone on the wet sidewalk. A few cars passed without slowing. He couldn't hear her, could only see her shrinking pale white face twisted in anguish and bobbing unevenly behind him in the rearview mirror.

ACKNOWLEDGMENTS

I deeply thank Bryan Hurt, Alexis Landau, Katherine Karlin, Chris Hackman, Mawi Asgedom, Kirsten Bohlman Heine, Jeremy Chignell, and all of my teachers at the University of Southern California, and in Los Angeles, especially John D. Buksbazen, Karin, Emily Hodgson Anderson, Aimee Bender, Percival Everett, Leo Braudy, George Wilson, TC Boyle, Hilary Schor, and Brad Pasanek. Thanks to USC and The Colorado College for commitment to the arts, to Kate Johnson and Barbara Galletly and everyone at Georges Borchardt, and to Judith Gurewich. Perpetual thanks to Ronald Piro, James Langlas, Jim McDonnell, Dale Jamieson, and David Mason, extraordinary teachers of beauty.